# MAJIPOOR—MENACED!

The ████████████████████████████
mirac██████████████████████████████
peopl██████████████████████████████
Bryna██████████████████████████████
lease will plunge the pla███████████

Valentine's lieutenant, Parras, has only thirty
days to find the child and stop the conspiracy.
Traveling undercover, Parras and the psychic Cylene must run a gauntlet of murderers, assassins,
intrigue and lies, to penetrate the hidden council
of the Metamorph Riurivars. Anyone they meet—
reptilian Ghayrogs, telepathic Vroons, three-eyed
Liimen, froglike Hjorts, giant Skandars—may be
with the enemy.

And Lord Valentine's enemies are not who—or
even *what*—they seem . . .

CROSSROADS™ ADVENTURES are authorized in-
teractive novels compatible for Advanced Dungeons and Dragons™ level play. Constructed by
the masters of modern gaming, CROSSROADS™
feature complete rules; *full use* of gaming values
—strength, intelligence, wisdom/luck, constitution, dexterity, charisma and hit points; and multiple pathways for each option; for the most
complete experience in gaming books, as fully
realized, motivated heroes quest through the most
famous worlds of fantasy!

## All-new. With an introduction by ROBERT SILVERBERG

## ENTER THE ADVENTURE!

## TOR'S CROSSROADS™ ADVENTURE SERIES

## COMING SOON

# A CROSSROADS™ ADVENTURE

## in the World of
## ROBERT SILVERBERG'S MAJIPOOR

# REVOLT ON MAJIPOOR

by
Matt Costello

A TOM DOHERTY ASSOCIATES BOOK

REVOLT ON MAJIPOOR

Copyright © 1987 by Bill Fawcett and Associates

First printing: August 1987

A TOR Book

Published by Tom Doherty Associates, Inc.
49 West 24 Street
New York, N.Y. 10010

Cover art by Doug Beekman
Illustrations by Todd Cameron Hamilton

ISBN: 0-812-56402-2
CAN. ED.: 0-812-56403-0

Printed in the United States of America

0 9 8 7 6 5 4 3 2 1

# DEDICATION

**To Ann, who also admired Parras**

# A CROSSROADS ADVENTURE

in the World of
## ROBERT SILVERBERG'S MAJIPOOR

# REVOLT ON MAJIPOOR

# MAJIPOOR:
# AN INTRODUCTION
## by Robert Silverberg

IT WAS THREE or four years since I had last written anything and I felt quite comfortable about that. I was busy traveling and reading and constructing an elaborate exotic garden at my northern California home, and those activities seemed quite sufficient for me. But then one warm April afternoon in 1978 as I was wandering around alone near my swimming pool I heard the old familiar voice in my head whispering things to me, and suddenly a new book was there. I went into my office and scribbled this on the back of an envelope:

The scene is a giant planet-sized city—an urban Big Planet, population of billions, a grand gaudy romantic canvas. The city is divided into vast subcities, each with its own characteristic tone. The novel is joyous and huge—no sense of dystopia. The form is that of a pilgrimage across the entire sphere. (For what purpose?) A colossal odyssey through bizarre bazaars. Parks and wonders.

I looked at that for a long moment and wondered if I really wanted to get myself mixed up in writing another book. Then I took a deep breath and added:

The book must be fun. Picaresque characters. Strange places—but all light, delightful, raffish. Magical mystery tour.

And then finally I scrawled:

Young man journeying to claim an inheritance that has been usurped. His own identity has been stolen and he now wears another body.

That was all I needed. The story was clear in my mind, and I felt an impulse saying, "Go on. Go ahead. Do it, you dope. *Do* it!" At the top of the envelope I wrote a title: *Lord Valentine's Castle*. And the next day I set about the process of finding a publisher for it. Before long contracts were being signed, and I was back at the typewriter (in those far-off days before word processors!) again after my long layoff, and the world of Majipoor began to come into existence.

\* \* \*

As Majipoor evolved in my mind, I realized that it couldn't all be covered by a single gigantic city, which had been my original conception. There had to be forests and valleys, mountains and deserts, agricultural zones, and such. Nevertheless I stuck to my basic notion of a gigantic planet that had a population of many billions, most of them living in enormous cities of great beauty and fascination. In order for human beings to live comfortably on so huge a planet, the gravitational pull has to be something reasonably similar to that of Earth—which meant a light core for Majipoor, very little in the way of metals. Metal-poor Majipoor therefore could not be a high-technology planet. Since it exists some fifteen or twenty thousand years in our future, it is able to take advantage of technological breakthroughs that are sheer magic to us, and so there is enough in the way of transportation, communications, and sanitation to provide a comfortable existence for its billions of inhabitants. Food is abundant, the air is fresh, the streams and oceans are clean. It is a cheerful and playful place in general, although highly urbanized. But in many respects it's an almost medieval place.

Majipoor was settled by colonists from Earth some fourteen thousand years ago, but also is occupied peacefully by representatives of a number of the galaxy's other intelligent species.

The chief alien life-forms that inhabit Majipoor are these:

—**Skandars.** Towering shaggy six-limbed beings of formidable strength and coordination, that look something like bears that walk upright and have four arms. They come from a chillier planet than Majipoor.

—**Ghayrogs.** Sleek reptilian-looking bipeds with scales and Medusa-like snaky hair.

—**Vroons.** Small many-tentacled creatures, a little like land-going octopuses in form, with telepathic powers.

—**Liimen.** Three-eyed humanoid creatures that live by farming or menial labor.

—**Hjorts.** Plump gray-skinned beings with frog-like eyes, frequently found in positions of minor authority (gatekeepers, customs officials, etc.).

Majipoor has, in addition, its own native intelligent race, the Piurivars, known to the settlers as shapeshifters or Metamorphs. These somewhat sinister humanoids, who are capable of physical changes of appearance, were rounded up long ago and forced to live in a reservation in an otherwise uninhabited part of the planet; they are regarded with some uneasiness by the settlers, who fear them for good reason.

One entire hemisphere of Majipoor is occupied by ocean—the Great Sea, which is so vast that no explorers have ever crossed it in its entirety. (In general the people of Majipoor are not given to making difficult and risky expeditions without purpose, and few can see any purpose in sailing across the immensity of the Great Sea.) The most conspicuous inhabitants of the ocean are known as sea-dragons—gigantic creatures that move in immense migratory herds across the entire planet. The other hemisphere is occupied by three continents of huge size and a smaller, though not insignificant, island located at the center of the Inner Sea between the continents. These are:

**—Alhanroel.** The first of the continents to be settled, and the one with the largest population. The main governmental center is here, at Castle Mount, a gigantic mountain thirty miles high that has hundreds of cities located on its climate-controlled slopes. In the center of Alhanroel is a second governmental center, the Labyrinth, an underground city constructed in the form of a many-leveled maze.

**—Zimroel.** A rich and fertile continent bisected by the River Zimr, which runs from west to east through its upper third. Such major cities as the river port of Ni-Moya and the ocean ports of Pidruid (in the west) and Piliplok (in the east) are found here. In the center of the continent is the Metamorph Reservation, closed to all outsiders.

**—Suvrael.** This southern continent is virtually all desert, though some areas are suitable for grazing animals. Its few cities are found along its northern coast.

The large island in the middle of the Inner Sea is known as the Isle of Dreams. It is the religious center of the planet.

The governmental system of Majipoor is a complex elective monarchy overseeing a hereditary aristocracy. Its chief figures are:

**—The Pontifex.** An imperial figure, aloof and virtually unknowable, who has no direct contact with those he rules. Surrounded by a great entourage, the Pontifex dwells in his palace in the depths of the Labyrinth on Alhanroel and rarely if ever emerges. No one speaks directly to him; he is addressed in the third person by a court official who relays the statements of others to him.

**—The Coronal.** He is the heir apparent to the Pontifex, and is generally a man of young or early middle years. The Coronal is the chief administrative officer of the realm, a combination of field marshal and prime minister, a person of vigor and decisiveness. He is considered to be the adoptive son of the reigning Pontifex and is chosen by him from a cadre of specially trained candidates who reside on Castle Mount. Upon the death of the Pontifex the Coronal succeeds him, entering the Labyrinth to stay and naming a new Coronal.

**—The Lady of the Isle of Sleep.** She is high priestess of the realm, virtually a mother-goddess figure as well. From her island sanctuary she presides over the spiritual life of the planet, appearing in dreams to citizens and guiding them toward higher aspirations—a process made possible through technological means. She is more often invoked as a symbol of virtue than actually involved in direct political activity. The Lady of the Isle is usually the mother of the reigning Coronal, and when he succeeds to the Pontificate she customarily retires in favor of the mother of the new Coronal, although she may retain her post if the new Coronal is motherless. Any vacancy in the Ladyship can also be filled from among her associated priestesses.

**—The King of Dreams.** This dark and powerful figure occupies an ambiguous role in the hierarchy, often opposing the decrees of the Pontifex and thwarting the actions of the Coronal. His power, which was established more recently than that of the other three high officials, derives from his control of thought-amplifying apparatus more potent than that used by the Lady of the Isle of Sleep. While she can make suggestions that guide and direct, his machinery is capable of controlling. Customarily he serves as the executive arm of the Pontifex/Coronal administration, but when he chooses to defy them he can cause considerable trouble. The office of the King of Dreams is hereditary and has remained within the family of the Barjazids since its inception.

The enormous planet of Majipoor is a wonderful and beautiful place, filled with strange plants and animals, spectacular scenic areas, marvelous cities of a size almost beyond comprehension. In the fourteen thousand years of human settlement there, all manner of astonishing things have happened—and there is plenty to come.

# INTRODUCTION AND RULES TO CROSSROADS™ ADVENTURES
## Bill Fawcett

FOR THE MANY of us who have enjoyed the stories upon which this adventure is based, it may seem a bit strange to find an introduction this long at the start of a book. What you are holding is both a game and an adventure. Have you ever read a book and then told yourself you would have been able to think more clearly or seen a way out of the hero's dilemma? In a Crossroads™ adventure you have the opportunity to do just that. *You* make the key decisions. By means of a few easily followed steps you are able to see the results of your choices.

A Crossroads™ adventure is as much fun to read as it is to play. It is more than just a game or a book. It is a chance to enjoy once more a familiar and treasured story. The excitement of adventuring in a beloved universe is neatly blended into a story which stands well on its own merit, a story in which you will encounter many familiar characters and places and discover more than a few new ones as well. Each adventure is a thrilling tale, with the extra suspense and satisfaction of knowing that you will succeed or fail by your own endeavors.

## THE ADVENTURE

Throughout the story you will have the opportunity to make decisions. Each of these decisions will affect whether *the hero* succeeds in the quest, or even survive. In some cases you will actually be fighting battles; other times you will use your knowledge and instincts to choose the best path to follow. In many cases there will be clues in the story or illustrations.

A Crossroads™ adventure is divided into sections. The length of a section may be a few lines or many pages. The section numbers are shown at the top of a page to make it easier for you to follow. Each section ends when you must make a decision, or fight. The next section you turn to will show the results of your decision. At least one six-sided die and a pencil are needed to "play" this book.

The words "six-sided dice" are often abbreviated as "D6". If more than one is needed a number will precede the term. "Roll three six-

sided dice" will be written as roll "3 D6".
Virtually all the die rolls in these rules do
involve rolling three six-sided dice (or rolling
one six-sided die three times) and totaling what
is rolled.

If you are an experienced role play gamer,
you may also wish to convert the values given in
this novel to those you can use with TSR's
Advanced Dungeons and Dragons™ or any other
role playing game. All of the adventures have
been constructed so that they also can be easily
adapted in this manner. The values for the hero
will transfer directly. While AD & D™ games are
much more complicated, doing this will allow
you to be the Game Master for other players.
Important values for the hero's opponents will
be given to aid you in this conversion and to give
those playing by the Crossroads™ rules a better
idea of what they are facing.

## THE HERO

Seven values are used to describe the hero in
gaming terms. These are strength, intelligence,
wisdom/luck, constitution, dexterity, charisma,
and hit points. These values measure all of a
character's abilities. At the end of these rules is
a record sheet. On it are given all of the values
for the hero of this adventure and any equipment or supplies they begin the adventure with.

While you adventure, this record can be used to keep track of damage received and any new equipment or magical items acquired. You may find it advisable to make a photocopy of that page. Permission to do so, for your own use only, is given by the publisher of this game/novel. You may wish to consult this record sheet as we discuss what each of the values represents.

# STRENGTH

This is the measure of how physically powerful your hero is. It compares the hero to others in how much the character can lift, how hard he can punch, and just how brawny he is. The strongest a normal human can be is to have a strength value of 18. The weakest a child would have is a 3. Here is a table giving comparable strengths:

| Strength | Example |
|----------|---------|
| 3 | A five-year-old child |
| 6 | An elderly man |
| 8 | Out of shape and over 40 |
| 10 | An average 20-year-old man |
| 13 | In good shape and works out |
| 15 | A top athlete or football running back |
| 17 | Changes auto tires without a jack |
| 18 | Arm wrestles Arnold Schwarzenegger and wins |

A Tolkien-style troll, being magical, might have a strength of 19 or 20. A full-grown elephant has a strength of 23. A fifty-foot dragon would have a strength of 30.

# INTELLIGENCE

Being intelligent is not just a measure of native brain power. It is also an indication of the ability to use that intelligence. The value for intelligence also measures how aware the character is, and so how likely they are to notice a subtle clue. Intelligence can be used to measure how resistant a mind is to hypnosis or mental attack. A really sharp baboon would have an intelligence of 3. Most humans (we all know exceptions) begin at about 5. The highest value possible is an 18. Here is a table of relative intelligence:

| Intelligence | Example |
| --- | --- |
| 3 | My dog |
| 5 | Lassie |
| 6 | Curly (the third Stooge) |
| 8 | Somewhat slow |
| 10 | Average person |
| 13 | College professor/good quarterback |
| 15 | Indiana Jones/Carl Sagan |
| 17 | Doc Savage/Mr. Spock |
| 18 | Leonardo da Vinci (Isaac Asimov?) |

Brainiac of comicbook fame would have a value of 21.

## WISDOM/LUCK

Wisdom is the ability to make correct judgments, often with less than complete facts. Wisdom is knowing what to do and when to do it. Attacking, when running will earn you a spear in the back, is the best part of wisdom. Being in the right place at the right time can be called luck or wisdom. Not being discovered when hiding can be luck, if it is because you knew enough to not hide in the poison oak, wisdom is also a factor. Activities which are based more on instinct, the intuitive leap, than analysis are decided by wisdom.

In many ways both wisdom and luck are further connected, especially as wisdom also measures how friendly the ruling powers of the universe (not the author, the fates) are to the hero. A hero may be favored by fate or luck because he is reverent or for no discernible reason at all. This will give them a high wisdom value. Everyone knows those "lucky" individuals who can fall in the mud and find a gold coin. Here is a table measuring relative wisdom/luck:

| Wisdom | Example |
|--------|---------|
| Under 3 | Cursed or totally unthinking |
| 5 | Never plans, just reacts |

| 7  | Some cunning, "street smarts" |
| 9  | Average thinking person |
| 11 | Skillful planner, good gambler |
| 13 | Successful businessman/Lee Iacocca |
| 15 | Captain Kirk (wisdom)/Conan (luck) |
| 17 | Sherlock Holmes (wisdom)/Luke Skywalker (luck) |
| 18 | Lazarus Long |

# CONSTITUTION

The more you can endure, the higher your constitution. If you have a high constitution you are better able to survive physical damage, emotional stress, and poisons. The higher your value for constitution, the longer you are able to continue functioning in a difficult situation. A character with a high constitution can run farther (though not necessarily faster) or hang by one hand longer than the average person. A high constitution means you also have more stamina, and recover more quickly from injuries. A comparison of values for constitution:

| Constitution | Example |
| --- | --- |
| 3 | A terminal invalid |
| 6 | A ten-year-old child |
| 8 | Your stereotyped "98 pound weakling" |
| 10 | Average person |
| 14 | Olympic Athlete/Sam Spade |

| 16 | Marathon runner/Rocky |
| 18 | Rasputin/Batman |

A whale would have a constitution of 20. Superman's must be about 50.

# DEXTERITY

The value for dexterity measures not only how fast a character can move, but how well-coordinated those movements are. A surgeon, a pianist, and a juggler all need a high value for dexterity. If you have a high value for dexterity you can react quickly (though not necessarily correctly), duck well, and perform sleight of hand magic (if you are bright enough to learn how). Conversely, a low dexterity means you react slowly and drop things frequently. All other things being equal, the character with the highest dexterity will have the advantage of the first attack in a combat. Here are some comparative examples of dexterity:

| Dexterity | Example |
| --- | --- |
| 3 or less | Complete klutz |
| 5 | Inspector Clousseau |
| 6 | Can walk and chew gum, most of the time |
| 8 | Barney Fife |
| 10 | Average person |
| 13 | Good fencer/Walter Payton |
| 15 | Brain surgeons/Houdini |

| 16 | Flying Karamazov Brothers |
| 17 | Movie ninja/Cyrano de Bergerac |
| 18 | Bruce Lee |

Batman, Robin, Daredevil and The Shadow all have a dexterity of 19. At a dexterity of 20 you don't even see the man move before he has taken your wallet and underwear and has left the room (the Waco Kid).

# CHARISMA

Charisma is more than just good looks, though they certainly don't hurt. It is a measure of how persuasive a hero is and how willing others are to do what he wants. You can have average looks yet be very persuasive, and have a high charisma. If your value for charisma is high, you are better able to talk yourself out of trouble or obtain information from a stranger. If your charisma is low, you may be ignored or even mocked, even when you are right. A high charisma value is vital to entertainers of any sort, and leaders. A different type of charisma is just as important to spies. In the final measure a high value for charisma means people will react to you in the way you desire. Here are some comparative values for charisma:

| Charisma | Example |
| 3 | Hunchback of Notre Dame |

| | |
|---|---|
| 5 | An ugly used car salesman |
| 7 | Richard Nixon today |
| 10 | Average person |
| 12 | Team coach |
| 14 | Magnum, P.I. |
| 16 | Henry Kissinger/Jim DiGriz |
| 18 | Dr. Who/Prof. Harold Hill (Centauri) |

# HIT POINTS

Hit points represent the total amount of damage a hero can take before he is killed or knocked out. You can receive damage from being wounded in a battle, through starvation, or even through a mental attack. Hit points measure more than just how many times the hero can be battered over the head before he is knocked out. They also represent the ability to keep striving toward a goal. A poorly paid mercenary may have only a few hit points, even though he is a hulking brute of a man, because the first time he receives even a slight wound he will withdraw from the fight. A blacksmith's apprentice who won't accept defeat will have a higher number of hit points.

A character's hit points can be lost through a wound to a specific part of the body or through general damage to the body itself. This general damage can be caused by a poison, a bad fall, or even exhaustion and starvation. Pushing your body too far beyond its limits may result in a successful action at the price of the loss of a few hit points. All these losses are treated in the same manner.

Hit points lost are subtracted from the total on the hero's record sheet. When a hero has lost all of his hit points, then that character has failed. When this happens you will be told to which section to turn. Here you will often find a description of the failure and its consequences for the hero.

The hit points for the opponents the hero meets in combat are given in the adventure. You should keep track of these hit points on a piece of scrap paper. When a monster or opponent has lost all of their hit points, they have lost the fight. If a character is fighting more than one opponent, then you should keep track of each of their hit points. Each will continue to fight until it has 0 hit points. When everyone on one side of the battle has no hit points left, the combat is over.

Even the best played character can lose all of his hit points when you roll too many bad dice during a combat. If the hero loses all of his hit points the adventure may have ended in failure. You will be told so in the next section you are instructed to turn to. In this case you can turn back to the first section and begin again. This time you will have the advantage of having learned some of the hazards the hero will face.

# TAKING CHANCES

There will be occasions where you will have to decide whether the hero should attempt to perform some action which involves risk. This might be to climb a steep cliff, jump a pit, or juggle three daggers. There will be other cases where it might benefit the hero to notice something subtle or remember an ancient ballad perfectly. In all of these cases you will be asked to roll three six-sided dice (3 D6) and compare the total of all three dice to the hero's value for the appropriate ability.

For example, if the hero is attempting to juggle three balls, then for him to do so successfully you would have to roll a total equal to or less than the hero's value for dexterity. If your total was less than this dexterity value, then you would be directed to a section describing how the balls looked as they were skillfully juggled. If you rolled a higher value than that for dexterity, then you would be told to read a section which describes the embarrassment of dropping the balls, and being laughed at by the audience.

Where the decision is a judgment call, such as whether to take the left or right staircase, it is left entirely to you. It will be likely somewhere in the adventure or in the original novels there will be some piece of information which would indicate that the left staircase leads to a trap and the right to your goal. No die roll will be needed for a judgment decision.

In all cases you will be guided at the end of each section as to exactly what you need do. If you have any questions you should refer back to these rules.

# MAGICAL ITEMS AND SPECIAL EQUIPMENT

There are many unusual items which appear in the pages of this adventure. When it is possible for them to be taken by the hero, you will be given the option of doing so. One or more of these items may be necessary to the successful completion of the adventure. You will be given the option of taking these at the end of a section. If you choose to pick up an item and succeed in getting it, you should list that item on the hero's record sheet. There is no guarantee that deciding to take an item means you will actually obtain it. If someone owns it already they are quite likely to resent your efforts to take it. In some cases things may not even be all they appear to be or the item may be trapped or cursed. Having it may prove a detriment rather than a benefit.

All magical items give the hero a bonus (or penalty) on certain die rolls. You will be told when this applies, and often given the option of whether or not to use the item. You will be instructed at the end of the section on how many points to add to or subtract from your die roll. If you choose to use an item which can function only once, such as a magic potion or hand grenade, then you will also be instructed to remove the item from your record sheet. Certain items, such as a magic sword, can be used many times. In this case you will be told when you obtain the item when you can apply the bonus. The bonus for a magic sword could be added every time a character is in hand-to-hand combat.

Other special items may allow a character to fly, walk through fire, summon magical warriors, or many other things. How and when they affect play will again be told to you in the paragraphs at the end of the sections where you have the choice of using them.

Those things which restore lost hit points are a special case. You may choose to use these at any time during the adventure. If you have a magical healing potion which returns 1 D6 of lost hit points, you may add these points when you think it is best to. This can even be during a combat in the place of a round of attack. No matter how many healing items you use, a character can never have more hit points than they begin the adventure with.

There is a limit to the number of special items any character may carry. In any Crossroads™ adventure the limit is four items. If you already have four special items listed on your record sheet, then one of these must be discarded in order to take the new item. Any time you erase an item off the record sheet, whether because it was used or because you wish to add a new item, whatever is erased is permanently lost. It can never be "found" again, even if you return to the same location later in the adventure.

Except for items which restore hit points, the hero can only use an item in combat or when given the option to do so. The opportunity will be listed in the instructions.

In the case of an item which can be used in every combat, the bonus can be added or subtracted as the description of the item indicates. A +2 sword would add two points to any total rolled in combat. This bonus would be used each and every time the hero attacks. Only one attack bonus can be used at a time. Just because a hero has both a +1 and a +2 sword doesn't mean he knows how to fight with both at once. Only the better bonus would apply.

If a total of 12 is needed to hit an attacking monster and the hero has a +2 sword, then you will only need to roll a total of 10 on the three dice to successfully strike the creature.

You could also find an item, perhaps enchanted armor, which could be worn in all combat and would have the effect of subtracting its bonus from the total of any opponent's attack on its wearer. (Bad guys can wear magic armor, too.) If a monster normally would need a 13 to hit a character who has obtained a set of +2 armor, then the monster would now need a total of 15 to score a hit. An enchanted shield would operate in the same way, but could never be used when the character was using a weapon which needed both hands, such as a pike, long-bow or two-handed sword.

## COMBAT

There will be many situations where the hero will be forced, or you may choose, to meet an opponent in combat. The opponents can vary from a wild beast, to a human thief, or an unearthly monster. In all cases the same steps are followed.

The hero will attack first in most combats unless you are told otherwise. This may happen when there is an ambush, other special situations, or because the opponent simply has a much higher dexterity.

At the beginning of a combat section you will be given the name or type of opponent involved. For each combat five values are given. The first of these is the total on three six-sided dice needed for the attacker to hit the hero. Next to this value is the value the hero needs to hit these opponents. After these two values is listed the hit points of the opponent. If there is more than one opponent, each one will have the same number. (See the Hit Points section included earlier if you are unclear as to what these do.)

Under the value needed to hit by the opponent is the hit points of damage that it will do to the hero when it attacks successfully. Finally, under the total needed for the hero to successfully hit an opponent is the damage he will do with the different weapons he might have. Unlike a check for completing a daring action (where you wish to roll under a value), in a combat you have to roll the value given or higher on three six-sided dice to successfully hit an opponent.

For example:

Here is how a combat between the hero armed with a sword and three brigands armed only with daggers is written:

**BRIGANDS**

| | | |
|---|---|---|
| *To hit the hero: 14* | *To be hit: 12* | *Hit points: 4* |
| *Damage with* | *Damage with* | |
| *daggers: 1 D6* | *sword: 2 D6* | |
| *(used by the* | *(used by the hero)* | |
| *brigands)* | | |

*There are three brigands. If two are killed (taken to 0 hit points) the third will flee in panic.*

*If the hero wins, turn to section 85.*

*If he is defeated, turn to section 67.*

# RUNNING AWAY

Running rather than fighting, while often

desirable, is not always possible. The option to run away is available only when listed in the choices. Even when this option is given, there is no guarantee the hero can get away safely.

# THE COMBAT SEQUENCE

Any combat is divided into alternating rounds. In most cases the hero will attack first. Next, surviving opponents will have the chance to fight back. When both have attacked, one round will have been completed. A combat can have any number of rounds and continues until the hero or his opponents are defeated. Each round is the equivalent of six seconds. During this time all the parties in the combat may actually take more than one swing at each other.

The steps in resolving a combat in which the hero attacks first are as follows:

1. Roll three six-sided dice. Total the numbers showing on all three and add any bonuses from weapons or special circumstances. If this total is the same or greater than the second value given, "to hit the opponent," then the hero has successfully attacked.

2. If the hero attacks successfully, the next step is to determine how many hit points of

damage he did to the opponent. The die roll for this will be given below the "to hit opponent" information.

3. Subtract any hit points of damage done from the opponent's total.

4. If any of the enemy have one or more hit points left, then the remaining opponent or opponents now can attack. Roll three six-sided dice for each attacker. Add up each of these sets of three dice. If the total is the same or greater than the value listed after "to hit the hero" in the section describing the combat, the attack was successful.

5. For each hit roll the number of dice listed for damage. Subtract the total from the number of hit points the hero has at that time. Enter the new, lower total on the hero's record sheet.

If both the hero and one or more opponents have hit points left, the combat continues. Start again at step one. The battle ends only when the hero is killed, all the opponents are killed or all of one side has run away. A hero cannot, except through a healing potion or spells or when specifically told to during the adventure, regain lost hit points. A number of small wounds from several opponents will kill a character as thoroughly as one titanic, unsuccessful combat with a hill giant.

## DAMAGE

The combat continues, following the sequence given below, until either the hero or his opponents have no hit points. In the case of multiple opponents, subtract hit points from one opponent until the total reaches 0 or less. Extra hit points of damage done on the round when each opponent is defeated are lost. They do not carry over to the next enemy in the group. To win the combat, you must eliminate all of an opponent's hit points.

The damage done by a weapon will vary depending on who is using it. A club in the hands of a child will do far less damage than the same club wielded by a hill giant. The maximum damage is given as a number of six-sided dice. In some cases the maximum will be less than a whole die. This is abbreviated by a minus sign followed by a number. For example, D6−2, meaning one roll of a six-sided dice, minus two. The total damage can never be less than zero, meaning no damage done. 2 D6−1 means that you should roll two six-sided dice and then subtract one from the total of them both.

A combat may, because of the opponent involved, have one or more special circumstances. It may be that the enemy will surrender

or flee when its hit point total falls below a
certain level, or even that reinforcements will
arrive to help the bad guys after so many
rounds. You will be told of these special situations in the lines directly under the combat
values.

Now you may turn to section one.

# RECORD SHEET

**PARRAS CORBALIN, lieutenant and personal aide to Lord Valentine of Majipoor.**

---

Strength:   16
Intelligence:   14
Wisdom:   11
Constitution:   13
Dexterity:   14
Charisma:   12


Hit Points:   18


Equipment:   A pack with 3 days' food, change of clothes, and 11 Crowns.

Weapon Carried:   Vibration Sword (1 D6 Damage).

---

\* **1** \*

First it grows colder, the wind biting into Parras as he climbs on the ice-covered upper slope of Mt. Zygnor. He clings to the ropes pinned to the rock while standing on two pitons that somehow support his great weight. His back is to the Great Sea, only occasionally visible as the heavy clouds part to reveal it, dark and gray in the morning light.

Now the ice begins to build up, collecting first on Parras' well-insulated gloves and then on his goggles, rendering everything a crystalline blur.

He must keep climbing, he knows. To stop now, to wait until the clouds lift, is to wait for death.

He moves his hand, reaching into a sack lashed to his side. He flexes his fingers to clear the hand of ice, and then he digs out another piton. Letting the safety ropes hold him fast, he grabs the hammer and pounds the piton well above his head, hoping that hard grylite does not suddenly give way to a more porous rock.

He hits as hard as he can, aware of the growing chunks of ice building on his boots. One, then another, metal piton is pounded into the dense, bluish rock. Parras reaches up to grab the pitons, and then he pushes gently upward with the toes of his boots, now not able to see anything, feeling only the icy intimacy of the cliff face.

But one piton comes flying out, and all of a sudden Parras is spinning around, facing out, now, away from the mountain, ready to slide down. He counts. If the other piton holds until the count of ten, he tells himself, it will give him a chance.

If not . . . if not—

"One," he says aloud. Then, trying not to hurry, "Two. Three. Four. Five." Was that some movement he felt? Perhaps the slightest tilting forward of the piton before it pops out, sending him tumbling down, easily pulling out the safety ropes attached to his belt?

"Six. Seven." It *is* holding, and if he was religious he would start muttering words to some deity who watches over fools who risk their lives. "Eight. Nine." He turns himself around, his cheek once again against the mountain, and then lowers himself back to his former handholds. His boots, too, find their resting place.

His heartbeat begins to slow and, forcing himself to concentrate, Parras tries to relax. And then he starts again. The pitons, the hammering, and again, until he is crawling up the cliff, blindly. He knows that to rush is foolish. And a mountain such as Zygnor does not suffer fools gladly.

He climbs up, until he feels the cliff yield, and

he knows it's over. A warm feeling of triumph fills him. He pulls himself up and, still unable to see, he crawls onto a ledge not more than three feet wide.

A place to rest, Parras thinks. Home, and he smiles, breaking the tiny icicles that dangle from his moustache.

He scrapes his goggles, clearing them, and then disconnects the safety lines attached to his belt, taking care to moor them to the ledge. After all, he does want to go down again. But for now there is only one thing. To stand here, at the top of Mt. Zygnor, the actual peak a mere twelve feet above, and below him all of Alhanroel. All, that is, except for Castle Mount, still many more miles higher, its hundreds of climate-controlled cities protected from these storms. Why, even now Parras knows that people on Castle Mount, at this very same height, are strolling through lush flower-filled gardens, listening to the hypnotic sound of the singing ferns in the warm morning air.

Which is why he is here in the first place. To taste something new, free from the perfect control of the Coronal's mountain.

Parras slides off his backpack and digs out the lightweight sleeping bag that will keep him warm during this tempest. He finds an opening in the rock and places a small quartz heater, still fully charged and ready to heat his tea. He unwraps some dried bilantoon meat and bites off a chunk. Salty and tangy to taste, Parras finds it oh-so-good to chew.

# Section 1

It was worth it, he reflects. Too many years on the Mount had dulled his senses. What was it Valentine had said to him? Peace can make a young man old before his time. And yet war can make that time all too short.

Parras takes another bite of the bilantoon, and lifts his metal cup from the heater. The different herbs from the tea fill his nostrils with familiar scents that remind him of his Lord Valentine and the Great Castle.

It was sheer luck that he became one of Valentine's personal lieutenants. Everyone fought fiercely the day Lord Valentine reclaimed his throne and threw down the Metamorph who ruled in his stead. It became a quest to save Majipoor, a quest that ended in a great celebration inside the Confalume throne room, the largest and grandest of the rooms in the castle. Its brightly gilded beams and colorful tapestries overwhelmed Parras, who had spent his days in the simple quarters of the Coronal's army.

But Valentine's hand singled him out, saying that his bravery, fighting beside Valentine and the incredible Skandar Zalzan Kavol, was something that must be rewarded. And so, Parras was appointed to stay beside Lord Valentine, the Coronal. As a lieutenant, an emissary, a confidant. It was a remarkable honor.

And also very boring.

The affairs of the kingdom, despite its sheer immensity, ran smoothly, requiring little directly of Lord Valentine and usually even less of his lieutenant, Parras Corbalin.

It took this, a risky, dangerous act such as climbing the great Zygnor alone, to sharpen his taste for a life sometimes lacking in flavor.

Suddenly, a high-pitched sound penetrates the thick layer of fur that surrounds Parras' ears. A message, he realizes, and one of the highest importance. Only one person knows where I am, thinks Parras. Only Valentine himself knows, and this message must be from him.

Parras quickly pulls a shiny black disk out of a side pocket of his pack, and then touches its edge in the proper sequence to receive the message. Though it comes from thousands of miles away, the voice is as clear as though Valentine himself stood on this ledge.

And the voice Parras hears is a grave one, lacking all traces of familiarity and lightness.

"Parras, you must return," Parras hears as the icy wind dances around him. "I would not trouble you if I was not in most urgent need."

"Yes, my lord," Parras responds, picking up on the formal tone of Valentine's voice.

"I need you at the Castle immediately. Rest as little as possible, talk to no one."

"It is as good as done," Parras answers.

The disk becomes quiet; the message is over.

And Parras leans over, looking down at the ice-covered face he thought he would not embrace again until the next, hopefully more sunny, morning.

©1986

We must touch again much sooner, he thinks. He dumps out the rest of his tea, and rolls the unused sleeping bag back into his pack. The small heater is still warm as he shoves it in with the rest of his gear, readying himself to climb down.

It's always harder to go down, he thinks. I tend to rush, going down. The pitons sometimes grow loose. Memory can play tricks on you, making you think that there's a crack here to stick your boot into, or there's a small ledge that you can grab with your hand.

Oh, yes, going down is so easy.

If you don't care how fast you go.

*Roll 3 D6.*

*If the roll is greater than Parras' Dexterity, turn to section 2.*

*If the roll is less than his Dexterity, turn to section 3.*

*If the roll is less than 6, turn to section 4.*

## * **2** *

Parras reaches out for a piton that's not there. He feels his body start to pull him down, while he wonders what happened. Was it someplace else, a little lower maybe, or a little more to the right? Or had it slipped out just after he got to the top, leaving nothing behind save a small hole?

All he knows is that he's holding on with one arm now.

*Roll 3 D6.*

*If the roll is greater than his value for Strength, turn to section 5.*

*If it is less than his value for Strength, turn to section 3.*

## * **3** *

Parras gradually locates his misplaced trail of pitons leading down, and he struggles to go slowly, gently easing himself down even as great chunks of hail snap at his back.

Then he searches with his boot for the bottom pitons, swinging his legs like pendulums, but feeling nothing.

*Roll 3 D6.*

*If it's greater than Parras' value for Strength, turn to section 5.*

*If it's less than Parras' value for Strength, turn to section 4.*

## * 4 *

Parras cautiously moves down the cliff face, thinking of only one thing, the next few inches. From one handhold to the next, re-attaching safety lines, checking the strength of each piton, and always straining every muscle to keep embracing the icy rock.

How long it takes him, he does not know. It is still light, though the exact location of Majipoor's sun is impossible to determine. He sees nothing, and the only sound is the wind slapping the rock, attempting to blow him off like some tenacious fly.

Parras reaches the bottom of the cliff, only a mere one hundred feet below the peak. Pausing to clean his goggles and gather up his ropes, he continues to climb downward, knowing that there is little to challenge him ahead. He takes a moment to dig out another piece of chewy bilantoon, and then keeps moving, wondering what could be so important that Valentine would summon him.

Majipoor has been at peace ever since that fateful day that Valentine reclaimed his throne. Then Valentine married his Carabella in a tremendous celebration that lasted a full week. All of Majipoor joined them, with each city trying to outdo the other in the splendor of its parties, or the pageantry of its parades.

On the wedding night itself every major city of Majipoor staged a fireworks display that went on into the early morning hours. And, of course, dignitaries from other worlds, even those not especially friendly to Majipoor, sent gifts of varying degrees of usefulness. A three-headed Milop, a delicacy, so it is said; an air bed, crafted of fine wood yet designed to make a gentle, warm mattress of air to sleep on; and jewels and gems that glimmered with every color in the universe.

But as great as Valentine's joy was on that day, it was nine months later that his heart became truly full, when Lady Carabella presented him with a son. He was a sharp-eyed baby whose cries echoed down the halls, and they called him Brynamir. Zalzan Kavol picked the boy up on the day he was born and, holding him tightly to his furry cheek, announced to one and all that the boy had the hands of a juggler.

And that was a mere five years ago.

Now, Parras thinks, something is very wrong, some crisis that scares even Lord Valentine, who is surely the bravest man Parras ever met.

Mt. Zygnor ends suddenly, the rock leading to a thick forest of gawky androdragma trees laced with vibrant patches of flowering alabandina. Parras loosens his hood and jacket, feeling astonishingly warm. It is many miles yet to the village of Bylek, but Parras feels invigorated just once again standing on level ground.

The miles pass without incident and, just as it grows dark, the cloud cover lifts, revealing a beautiful shade of purple dotted with only the brightest stars.

Parras reaches Bylek just as many of the villagers are going to sleep. He passes a uniformed Hjort, apparently watching over the sleepy streets, and Parras realizes that he must look strange indeed.

Then he sees a brightly lit building ahead and a sign proclaiming it to be The Red Blave, an inn. He walks in, eager for a cup of thokka wine and, perhaps, some meat fresher than that in his backpack. A few minutes is all he will take. A bit of refreshment, and then he'll find Polol.

The room is crowded, a densely packed wonder of all Majipoor's creatures. A table of Ghayrogs sits almost sullenly in the corner, looking like conspirators, punctuating their remarks with licks of their forked tongues. The table nearest them, well away due to the strong acrid

odor often given off by Ghayrogs—especially when drinking—is filled with Hjorts whose somber expression is belied by their throaty laughs.

"Back so soon, young fellow? Old Zygnor prove too much for your out-of-shape carcass?" The Skandar standing at the bar laughs as he continues to talk to Parras. "There is a small hill nearby that the children play on, perhaps that—"

The crowd watches Parras, some eager to see some violence, others fearing that their quiet conversations over ale might be over. Parras takes off his jacket, his vibrating sword strapped tightly to his side, glistening in the smoky light.

Parras walks over to the steely-eyed Skandar. "I knew you'd be here, you fat old rug." The bartender stands nearby, frozen. "A glass of your best thokka wine," Parras says. "And if you have some cold, fresh meat, perhaps some blave, bring that too. And another ale for my friend Tylan Polol."

The bartender nods nervously and begins to pour.

The Skandar smiles, then opens his arms to hug Parras. "Good to see you so soon, my friend."

As usual, Parras is non-plussed by his friend's gigantic hug. "Tylan, I want you to rest assured that I've been to the top of Zygnor." The crowd, seeing the imagined confrontation melt away,

## Section 4

resumes their various conversations. The bartender puts down a tall glass of bluish wine and a plate of sliced meat. Parras takes a warming sip and speaks quietly to the Skandar.

"I've been summoned to the Mount. Immediately. As soon as I've finished this plate, you can take me to the floater and we'll return—"

The Skandar lets out a great sigh, his four arms waving in exasperation. "And my hunting? What of that? This was to be recreation for me too, Parras."

Parras looks at the Skandar, a look he used rarely, only when he needed to remind Tylan Polol of their special responsibilities. "If Lord Valentine needs our help, then we will do everything we possibly can. Everything." The thokka wine had disappeared, and the bartender poured another. "You've secured the floater, I assume?"

"Yes," Polol says. "It's locked in an old farmhouse just outside the village."

"And no one saw you?"

"No one."

Good, thinks Parras. Their floater carries the starburst seal of Majipoor, and it's bound to attract attention and unwanted interest. While the kingdom might be at peace, the throne was not without its enemies.

"Then, let's be off. We can be at Castle Mount by daybreak."

"This way, then, Parras. I'll tell the innkeeper to hold our rooms and watch our gear. With luck, we'll be back before the end of the hunting season."

After some words, and a few passed crowns to the bartender, Polol leads Parras out of the inn and down the road, to the east. The village ends abruptly, and the valley opens up to expose the rich farmlands of the valley. They walk quickly, silently, until Polol says, "There! It's locked inside that old barn. The farmer asked me no questions."

"Then why is the door open?" Parras asks. Without a word, he and Polol quickly ready their weapons.

*If Parras decides to hide and watch the old barn, turn to section 10.*

*If he decides to enter the barn, turn to section 7.*

*If he sends Polol ahead to look it over, turn to section 13.*

## \* **5** \*

Parras feels his hand begin to slip and, before he knows what's happening, he's twisting over and over, pulling one safety line out completely. He falls now, straight down, thinking only one thought—

That the other line holds.

## Section 6

With a sudden jerk, it snaps taut, pulling on his side with an abrupt jolt that squeezes the wind out of him. He swings back and forth, parallel to the ground and unable to see if the bottom of the cliff is five or fifty feet away.

He waits until he comes to a stop, then he digs out a pin and hammers it in anywhere, just as long as he can grab it to spin himself around. Then he hammers another so that he can start again the arduous process of climbing down.

The awful moment comes when he has to detach his one safety line still affixed to the cliff. From now on, he's climbing free.

Not by choice, he thinks ruefully. The other safety rope dangles down from his belt, useless.

*Parras has suffered 2 hit points of damage in the fall. Turn to section 4.*

* **6** *

"Nice and safe," Parras says sarcastically. "Another few minutes and they may have damaged the floater permanently."

Polol pulls himself atop the gleaming vehicle. "Looks okay from here. Of course, we won't really know until we use it."

Parras throws his backpack into the rear of the floater. "For your sake, Tylan my friend, I hope everything is fine. It's a long walk to Castle Mount."

"I know," the Skandar says. "And nary a decent inn between here and there."

Polol is already activating the floater by pressing the buttons that provide power. "Shall I navigate?" Polol asks.

"Wrong. I want to get back by dawn, and I'm not too sure how many ales you've had. *I'll* navigate and you can pilot."

"Good," Polol says with a relaxed smile. "That's mostly automatic anyhow."

Parras sits next to Polol, and straps himself into the seat, covered with a luminescent leather made out of the hide of a young sea-dragon. Polol guides the floater out of the barn, gently easing it up higher as he reaches the open air.

"Deftly done, Tylan," Parras laughs.

"No problem, Parras." He turns the floater sharply south. "Next stop, Castle Mount."

*Turn to section 19.*

*Turn to section 19.*

\* **7** \*

Parras and the Skandar enter the barn quickly, their swords ready. A single torch inside the decaying barn illuminates a bizarre scene. Two men are clambering over the floater, giving it a

## Section 8

cautious, uncomprehending scrutiny. A fat Hjort stands beside the floater, apparently directing them. It takes only a moment for the trio to stop and see Parras.

The Hjort immediately raises a broad cutlass, while the two men go for knives strapped to their calves. And to Parras, it's quite clear that they're about to throw them.

*Decide whether Parras will deal with the two men or the Hjort. Then turn to section 12.*

* **8** *

"Your friend Polol can accompany you to Mayrtria. Seek out the small fishing vessel, the *Dark Sea*. Cylene will be there. By week's end you'll be at Zimroel. When you have rescued my son, or learned of his fate, signal me with your communication disk.

"And now, I must listen to my ministers scream for war. Good luck, Parras."

Parras bows to Valentine, and then turns and moves quickly ahead of Polol, leaving the great throne room.

*Turn to section 30.*

## * 9 *

From what Parras knows of Metamorphs, the whole scenario seems wrong. Parras decides to press Valentine on his feelings about the situation.

*Roll 3 D6.*

*If it's less than Parras' Intelligence, turn to section 15.*

*If it's more than Parras' Intelligence, turn to section 18.*

## * 10 *

They scurry beside an outcrop of bunch fungus, taking care not to step on any, which would send out a crunchy alarm.

"Ouch," Polol hisses, kneeling on a thorny vine.

"Quiet, Tylan," Parras whispers. "Look! There they are." Parras points to three figures

# Section 10

struggling with the floater, grunting as they try to pull it out of the barn.

"Good thing they can't get it to work," Polol says. "They'd be long gone."

"They'll wreck it at this rate. You head left, and I'll go right. We'll try to get closer to them. When you see me stand up, come out swinging."

"Oh good, a bit of confrontational diplomacy with the locals," Polol says as he scrambles away. Parras begins creeping in the other direction, watching the thieves pulling at the floater, still firmly planted in the barn.

He creeps closer, seeing now that two of them are scruffy-looking Humans, while a bloated Hjort seems to be directing them. One of the Humans is on top of the floater, poking around the controls.

Parras stands up, and he sees the Skandar rise quickly, his vibrating sword already slicing the air. They run toward the floater.

*Parras has +1 advantage in all attacks in this confrontation. Decide whether he will go toward the Humans or the Hjort first. Then, turn to section 12.*

# * **11** *

Parras surprises the Humans, who nonetheless respond quickly, reaching for their slim stilettos, preparing to throw them.

*Roll 3 D6.*

*If it's less than Parras' value for Dexterity, he gets two attacks on the first round. Otherwise he gets one attack while the two thieves prepare to throw their knives.*

THIEVES *(each)*
To hit Parras: 14   To be hit: 12   Hit points: 28
*Damage with thrown knife: 1 D6−1*

*After the first round they will flee the barn. The Skandar will have made short work of the Hjort, fighting with a ferocity that scares even Parras. The Hjort lumbers away as best it can, as Polol's laugh fills the barn. Turn to section 6.*

## * **12** *

*If Parras attacks the Hjort, leaving the Humans for Polol, turn to section 21.*

*If Parras attacks the Humans, leaving the Hjort for Polol, turn to section 11.*

## * **13** *

Parras waits, crouching low while Polol scrambles forward, his four arms helping him crawl quickly through the tall grass.

Moments later, and Polol returns, a bit breathless as he talks.

"There's three of them, Parras. A Hjort and two Humans. As best as I can make out, they're trying to haul the floater out. They may have damaged it."

Parras nods. "Then we best move fast."

*Parras has a +1 advantage in any attacks against the thieves. Turn to section 7.*

## * **14** *

*If Parras decides to rely on his Intelligence, turn to section 9.*

*If Parras decides to rely on his Wisdom, turn to section 20.*

## * **15** *

"But surely," Parras says excitedly, "the Metamorphs realize that you can't remove your forces, no matter if your son is involved."

Valentine raises his eyebrows. "Precisely my thought. But then, they must actually hope that I will start a war."

"The Metamorphs want a war?"

"Perhaps," says Valentine. "Or, perhaps someone else does. Whatever the answer is, you and Cylene will have to find out."

*Parras will have a +1 advantage for any Intelligence rolls for the rest of the adventure. Turn to section 8.*

# * **16** *

"My lord," Parras says quietly. "I'm sure that there is something that you're not telling me."

"Oh, you do." Valentine looks around the massive room, his voice echoing. "I make no secret of my sympathy for the shapeshifters. We occupy a planet that was once theirs. Still, that is the past and they could no more rule Majipoor than could a city full of Liimen. But this, this goes against everything I've ever learned about them. I feel," he says, his eye taking on a distant look, "there is something else going on here. I sense the hand of someone who is not a Metamorph. It's a feeling, but no more than that."

*Parras has a +1 advantage in any rolls against his value for Wisdom for the rest of the adventure. Turn to section 8.*

## * **17** *

Valentine looks away, as if his eyes could stare right through the many layers of castle walls.

"Is there any other information you have . . . perhaps from your spies?" Parras asks quietly, feeling Valentine's pain fill the massive room with an almost unbearable presence.

"Information?" Valentine laughs, even as he dabs at a tear glistening on his cheek. "No, Parras. Even the King of Dreams appears to be sleeping through this nightmare."

Valentine turns and looks directly at Parras. "Come, my loyal lieutenant. You must begin."

*Turn to section 8.*

## * 18 *

"If it comes to war," Parras says, "the Meta-morphs will surely lose."

"Yes," Valentine says weakly. "And that is why you must do what you can. To save my son, and perhaps stop the annihilation of a race."

*Turn to section 8.*

## * 19 *

"Wake up, Tylan," Parras says, leaning over to shake the Skandar's shoulder. "We're almost there."

Parras watches the Skandar grumble and growl in his half-sleep, his dangling arms stretching and coming to action in a way that always intrigues Parras. He could never imagine what it would be like to control four arms. How does one issue commands for four of them? he wonders. Which brushes the teeth, which one holds the fork? And, of course, there would be twice as much awkwardness in a situation where you just didn't know what to do with your hands.

And none of these questions, Parras realizes with a small smile, ever seem to concern his burly friend.

"Just napping, Parras." Parras watches Polol blink to alertness, as together they watch the wonders of Castle Mount in the morning.

The light is behind them, bathing the many levels of the Mount in a warm, golden glow. There, just below them, they see Peritole Pass, and just ahead lies Bombifale Plain and the High Morpin Road.

And all around them they see a chain of smaller, dark-hued mountains all merging into this one massive mountain that juts nearly into space. And the Fifty Cities of Majipoor that dot the Mount are all stirring to life, as the unique buildings catch the yellow light and sharpen it into a crystalline sparkle.

The air is warm, soothing, as it always is on Castle Mount, and a hundred different fragrances fill the air, as one garden rivals the next.

They pass over a crew of Liimen working a small cliffside lusavender-seed plantation. One of them pauses to glance up at the floater, his three eyes blinking independently, in no apparent order.

And finally, the Castle itself is before them, spires upon spires, glimmering walls that reach straight up, even higher than the mountain, and then arch to the side, seemingly defying gravity

# Section 19

itself. A few sluggish Hjorts stand near the opulent Main Gate, victims of the graveyard shift, and they take little notice as the floater enters the main courtyard, an area larger than many of Majipoor's towns.

"It is a good feeling being back," Tylan Polol grunts, "no matter what the emergency. Why even now I'd be hunting—"

"If you were out of bed," Parras laughs.

Parras eases the floater down, noticing that a small contingent of the palace guard are standing around, obviously waiting for them. The floater comes to a stop.

"Lord Valentine is in the Confalume Throne Room," a chunky sergeant says, even as Parras and Tylan are stepping out of the floater. And then, in a lower voice, he adds, "He's been waiting all night."

They move briskly, making their way through the maze of corridors and rooms with an unerring sense of direction born of many years at the castle.

And, while walking, Parras wonders, Why the throne room? It's certainly not a place suited to a confidential matter of state.

Two Skandars, veterans of Lord Valentine's great march up the mountain, see them approach and open the two oaken doors to the throne room. Parras and Polol pick up their pace, sensing the urgency more intensely than before.

They enter, and there, standing under a tapestry detailing one of the final battles in the war with the Metamorphs, is Valentine. His eyes are dark, sunken, set in a face pulled tight with, what? Anger? Grief? Parras cannot tell.

"My Lord," Parras says, kneeling, and Polol joins him.

"Thank you for your speed, Parras. When I talk to you you'll know why every minute is important."

With a gesture, Valentine signals them to rise. Parras watches Valentine pour an amber liqueur from a clear flask. Powerful stuff for a breakfast drink, Parras thinks.

"In a few moments my advisors will enter, and the affairs of state will take . . . a more formal course. We have just this time now to see if something can be done, about this."

Valentine picks up a sheet of paper and hands it to Parras. He reads it:

Coronal!

Your son, Brynamir, has been taken by the nation of Piurivar. He is alive and well, and will remain so. You have one month to order the removal of all your forces from Zimroel. At that time, our representatives will assume control of the continent, as the separate nation of Piurivar.

Give the order, and your son will be returned. Failing that, your son will be put to death. We will then select another target from the foul families of Majipoor.

Piurivar. The Metamorphs' name for Majipoor, Parras thinks. "But how?" he asks, handing the note back.

"How?" Valentine sneers. "Isn't everything possible for a shapeshifter? Why," he says with an almost hateful bark, "perhaps even you—"

"My lord!"

"No. I know you are Parras. And only you can do what must be done." Valentine takes another deep sip of the liqueur, and then faces Parras. "Save my son. Only a mad splinter group could think that some lunatic scheme like this might work. Of course I can't honor their request. All of Majipoor would curse me forever, and rightly so. But if they . . . If my son is not returned, I'll have no choice but to wage war on the entire Metamorph Reservation. That too would be ordained.

"In fact, I'm sure many of my advisors will suggest doing that immediately, sending armies to eliminate the shapeshifters once and for all."

And Parras is overwhelmed by Valentine's pain. He hangs by a narrow thread, Parras senses. So close to snapping. "But what can I do?" Parras asks.

And Valentine's answer is ready.

"There are Metamorphs who would help stop this," Valentine says quietly, and Parras nods, knowing Valentine's sympathy for the former masters of the planet. "Find them, and get their help to recover my son before the month is out. After that time, it won't matter, for Majipoor's fate, and the fate of the Metamorphs, will be sealed."

"How can I get into the reservation?" Parras asks. "Won't I be stopped by—"

"You will travel by floater to Mayrtria, there to meet someone named Cylene. She is a scholar, very young, yet she knows more about the Metamorphs than anyone on the planet. You will leave your floater there, and your friend Polol—"

The Skandar looks up, a broad grimace of displeasure on his face.

Valentine continues. "You and Cylene will don the disguise of two researchers. You will travel by whatever means you can find, as fast as you can. Cylene should be able to gain entry into the reservation. Once there, you are to learn what you can. And, if it's nothing, in a little over thirty days, war will come to Majipoor."

Valentine pauses, walks over to Parras and puts a strong hand on his shoulder. "Not much time . . . an impossible task . . . a service to an old friend. Not an inconsiderable challenge, you'll agree. In fact, it may make the Zygnor seem like so much child's play."

Valentine holds Parras' gaze for a moment, his eyes lined with red streaks, as he fights for control.

## Sections 20, 21

*Decide whether Parras will leave now, or attempt to learn more from Valentine.*

*If Parras is ready to leave, turn to section 8.*

*If he continues to talk, turn to section 14.*

## \* **20** \*

Parras senses that there is more to be learned, and that there are other thoughts that Valentine might be able to share.

*If Parras rolls less than his value for Wisdom, turn to section 16.*

*If the total is more than Parras' value for Wisdom, turn to section 17.*

## \* **21** \*

Parras decides to go for the Hjort, leaving his many-armed friend to deal with the scruffy-looking thieves.

The Hjort moves quickly, belying his bloated

body, and moves to the side even as Parras comes straight at him.

HJORT
*To hit Parras: 13   To be hit: 11   Hit points: 8*
*Damage with cutlass: 1 D6*

*After one round of combat, turn to section 24.*

* **22** *

Cylene certainly seems to know what she wants, Parras thinks. But he doesn't exactly share her feelings regarding the shapeshifters. Cold, depthless creatures. Who could know what they feel? Still, it might be best to let her run the show, at least until they're in the reservation.

*Roll 3 D6.*

*If the total is the same or less than Parras' value for Wisdom, turn to section 27.*

*If the total is greater, turn to section 23.*

* **23** *

Cylene stands up and throws open a hidden compartment above her bunk.

"Put your sword in there," she orders.

Parras laughs. "What do you mean? I barely take the sword off to go to bed. And Zimroel is no place to be—"

"If you are seen wearing a sword," Cylene sighs, "it will let everyone know that you are no scholar. It must stay here. My father will see that it's kept safe until we return from the reservation. We are, after all, on a mission of peace."

She looks at Parras, as if it were impossible for him to say no.

*If Parras decides to hand her his weapon, turn to section 41.*

*If he decides to keep it, turn to section 36.*

## * **24** *

The Hjort's bulbous eyes widen in appreciation of Parras' skill with his sword, and he glances at the exit.

Parras sees the Hjort charge wildly at him, his cutlass swooping down, but then the Hjort quickly darts to the right, running out of the barn. Parras looks over to see whether Polol needs any help. One of the humans lies still, a great bloody stain spreading out from his midsection, and the Skandar appears to have a small wound on his chest.

The other human notices Parras and, seeing the Hjort gone, he scurries around to the back of the floater. By the time Parras reaches Polol the thief has already scrambled out a side window.

"That wasn't much of a workout," Polol laughs. Then, looking down at the corpse at his feet, "Except for this fellow."

Parras starts to examine the floater for damage.

*Turn to section 6.*

## * **25** *

It could be risky trusting Cylene's feelings about
Metamorphs, Parras realizes. Yet, he must depend on her, at least until they're inside the
reservation. After that, whatever it takes to rescue Valentine's son, and Majipoor, is the only
thing of importance.

*Roll 3 D6.*

*If the total is the same or less than Parras' value
for Intelligence, turn to section 32.*

*If the total is greater, turn to section 23.*

## * **26** *

There's a strange quality to this young woman,
some inner power that Parras senses. It's not, he
reflects, just the way she orders her father
around, or the way she helps run the ship.
    It's something else.
    She seemed to know who he was as soon as
she saw him. It's unnerving, Parras thinks, but
he feels almost exposed in front of her.

Perhaps, he wonders, there's another reason she was picked by Lord Valentine. For now, Parras would watch her carefully, to learn what he can.

*Parras will have a +1 advantage when using his skill of Charisma with Cylene. This advantage only applies to her. Turn to section 31.*

* **27** *

Yes, Parras tells himself, I must follow her. But I must keep my sword handy. She is a trusting soul, too trusting, and not experienced in the dangers of the world of politics.

And, Parras realizes, he now knows one reason for her self-assurance, her inner strength. Of course, he's suspected it all along.

She's a psychic.

And probably a pretty powerful one at that.

Something, to be sure, to keep in mind.

*Turn to section 23.*

# * **28** *

Perhaps it's a good time to smooth things out with Cylene, Parras realizes. After all, they will be spending a lot of time together, much of it traveling through the rough terrain of Zimroel.
   And besides, she's quite beautiful.

*Roll 3 D6.*

*If the total is the same or less than Parras' value for Charisma, turn to section 33.*

*If the total is greater, turn to section 23.*

# * **29** *

Is it a dream?
   Yes, his mind screams, that's all it is. It's just some foulness dredged up by the old King of Dreams himself, some terrible pain from dream-wounds. Yes, it's just a nightmare.
   But then it grows even darker, closing around him, engulfing him until he feels himself vanish, slowly becoming part of the emptiness that

surrounds him. And, in his last conscious moment, he's aware of a tiny, bright light, glimmering in some vast distance. And he races to it.

Parras is no more.

And what of Valentine, or his son, and the
Metamorphs, and the fate of Majipoor?

No Coronal of Majipoor would let the entire
hope of the planet rest on one person's shoulders, even one as loyal and strong as Parras.

There may yet be time . . .

*Parras has failed in this difficult challenge. You
may replay the adventure by raising Parras' skill
level (and hit points) by 1 point. If you wish to
begin the adventure at some point other than the
beginning, see the list of locations in section 110.*

## ✳ **30** ✳

It is still morning when they leave the endless
corridors of the castle, but almost all traces of
coolness are gone. They walk briskly toward
their floater, but Parras senses that his friend's
silence is merely the deceptive lull before the
raging storm begins.

He decides to brave Polol's rage.

"It was not my idea, Tylan. I, of course, would
want you to come."

The Skandar stops perfectly still, in the middle of the courtyard, his arms waving angrily. "But, begging his pardon, what is wrong with our good Lord Valentine?" Polol shouts. "Too much sipping on the thokka, perhaps? To think that he's sending you to a place where you could just vanish, disappear without a trace, thrown in some murky stream by shapeshifters. And *I* don't get to go. No, instead some woman will come along."

"He has reasons, Tylan, very—"

The Skandar brings an arm up to Parras' shoulder, and looks at his friend.

It's hard to read the message in such a shaggy face, Parras reflects. What is it saying now? Concern? Fear? Anger? Jealousy?

"If there's to be danger to you, I want to be there. Tell me, when have we ever faced enemies alone? Now, I'm to wait in Mayrtria while you adventure across the Inner Sea."

It's the fun, Parras thinks. That's it, most of it anyway. Polol just doesn't want to miss the excitement.

"It's Valentine's order, Tylan. And besides, do you think a Skandar could slip easily into the Metamorph Reservation? I have my doubts that I'll be able to, even posing as a scholar."

They were at the floater, watched now by only one guard. He backs away as Parras and Polol climb in. "Enough chatter, Parras. You have an appointment to keep. And I will get to do my hunting after all."

They take the floater up quickly, feeling almost as if they had never left it. Polol navigates now, plotting the most direct course and encoding the floater's memory, while Parras guides the copper-colored craft out of the courtyard, past the castle walls, and then down the tremendous mountain itself.

The journey to Mayrtria is uneventful, and Polol even begins to regain some of his composure. Halfway to Mayrtria he begins, once again, regaling Parras with his tales, most of them on the tall side, of female conquests in the bedrooms of Majipoor.

"Of course," he laughs, "I never have had a Ghayrog, though I've heard it's . . . possible." His whole furry belly shakes when he laughs. "A dozen teats may be an interesting experience. But to touch that leathery skin or smell those odors? Well, I'll pass on that, thank you. On the other hand, I knew this female Vroon once who worked, quite successfully, as a fortune-teller in Ni-Móya. With her six arms and my four, well, we made her small bed a mighty crowded place."

And on and on, Polol banters, drifting from conquest to conquest, misadventure to misadventure, and Parras knows that he will miss him greatly in the difficult quest ahead. And maybe, he wonders, he might not be the same person without Polol by his side. He's always been there, after all, to fight, to advise, or to just share his thoughts.

What now, Parras asks himself. What now?

# Section 30

After a few hours, they leave the lower hills that gird the Mount and, skirting the cities of Normork and Minimool, they enter the fertile region that begins at Bimbak West. Here begins the food supply for most of the inhabitants of Alhanroel. Mile after mile of niyk fields alternate with equally large farms devoted to glein or staaja. Parras takes the floater as low as he can so the rich smell of the crops surrounds them.

"In another life," Parras says quietly, "I would be a farmer."

"And I would be a thief and a rake," Polol laughs.

Then, as morning yields to early afternoon, they see the sparkling turquoise waters of the Inner Sea, and, just barely visible, the first buildings of Mayrtria. The simple, squat structures seem to Parras to belong to some other, less lush part of Majipoor.

"Certainly not the most beautiful of cities," Parras says.

"True enough," Polol agrees. "But it does have one first-class inn, at the northern end. I once met—"

"We're to proceed directly to the harbor, and the *Dark Sea*."

The Skandar harrumphed. "I was talking of later, when you're gone."

The residents of Mayrtria all stopped to watch the Coronal's floater as it sails overhead, an uncommon sight, moving now at a more stately pace. Devoted to the business of shipping crops, Parras knows, Mayrtria is not considered one of the jewels of Majipoor. A rather large proportion of its citizens are Ghayrogs who take a no-nonsense approach to their business.

The harbor appears suddenly, and Parras moves fast to slow the floater to avoid turning around in the rough sea wind. The hundreds of docks are largely empty. It's much too early in the season for the harvesting and shipping of crops to all the far-flung regions of Majipoor. A few docks show some sign of activity as machinery and raw materials are off-loaded.

"Pretty quiet, eh, Parras? Now, which of these bulky vessels do you suppose is the *Dark Sea*?"

Parras shakes his head. Short of examining each ship, he realizes he doesn't have a clue about how to find it.

Then Polol sees something, and signals Parras with a sharp tap on his arm. "Look there! Some Ghayrog is dressed in official clothes, there, standing beside that small hut. Perhaps he's an authority of some kind. Let's ask him."

Parras eases the floater down, right beside the Ghayrog, who seems to take no notice of the starburst seal. He merely flicks his tongue disinterestedly as Parras hops out.

"Good morning! We were wondering if you could give us some information."

The Ghayrog looks up slowly, the snake-like tendrils on his head slowly writhing as if in response to the question. "This is not," he says quietly, "the bureau of tourism. I suggest that you—"

Polol thrusts himself forward, right up to the Ghayrog's damp snout, letting his own face react to the acrid odor of the creature. "Just tell us, my friend, where we might find the *Dark Sea*."

The Ghayrog seems to smile and then, with some appetizing licks of its tongue, it answers.

"Oh, it's the *Dark Sea* you want. Why, then, you've come to the right place, oh yes. Merely follow the harbor north to almost the very end. You can't miss the vessel, oh no. It's about the last ship there."

Polol backs away as the aroma of the Ghayrog becomes almost overpowering. "Thank you," Parras says, and he and Polol pull themselves back into the floater and head north.

"Some of these cities are lacking in respect for the seal of the Coronal," Polol grunts as they move to the end of the harbor.

"Just as long as they pay their taxes, Tylan. What else matters?"

While most of the berths are empty, they pass over a handful of large cargo vessels, mammoth ships with dozens of levels, surmounted with enormous light sails, all now furled, and with the storage space equal to many large warehouses. Some of the ships are like small cities themselves, offering a full spectrum of recreational activities for the crew, including games, shops, entertainment cubes, and, it's rumored, activities of a more basic sort.

The docks end abruptly.

"There's nothing here!" Polol yells. "There's no—"

But then he sees where Parras is looking, and, for a moment, they are both silent.

A small ship sits bobbing in the great swells of the Inner Sea. While outfitted with a light sail—a decidedly primitive one—the ship appears to be something out of a history book. Some small primitive fishing vessel, perhaps, or a patrol boat used to stop smugglers. A museum piece, Parras reflects. Entirely out of date.

"The *Dark Sea*," he says quietly.

He brings the floater down beside it. "Yes," Polol says broadly, "it really is best you go alone. I would, of course, only be in the way. And with such a sturdy vessel to get you across the sea, you'll have nothing to worry about." The Skandar laughs, as Parras shakes his head and gets out.

He walks over to the ship and looks around. No one is around, as far as he can see, though the ship appears ready to leave. It may be old, he reflects, but it appears well maintained.

"Hello?" he calls, but no one answers. "I'm going on," he announces to Polol. "You wait out there." Parras walks up the plank, its boards creaking loudly with each step. The ship bobs furiously, and Parras has trouble taking even a small step. "Hello? Is anybody—"

"You can stop right there."

# Section 30

Parras turns to see a small, gray-bearded man standing behind him. He has a small energy thrower pointed right at him. "I'm looking for the captain of the vessel," Parras says quietly.

The small man glances over at Polol. "Tell your friend to keep his arms at his side or you'll spend the rest of your days without a head."

"Stop moving, Tylan," Parras barks. Then, "I was sent here by Lord Valentine. The documents are here, in my pocket. I'm supposed to meet someone named—"

Then she appears, from the same small door that the captain used. She is small, not much over five feet tall, with deep blue eyes and a half-smile that spoke of secrets and sadness. She looks at Parras, then to the floater, noticing the seal of the Coronal.

"It's okay, Father," she says quietly, with an authority that surprises Parras. "They're the ones. You are . . ."

"Parras. And you must be Cylene."

"Yes," she says. "And we must hurry. Your room is aft. Small, but serviceable."

The old man lowers his energy thrower.

"But I'll need your help on deck," he orders, "so no hiding in your room. This ship may be old, but it can move fast."

Already Cylene is undoing the ropes that hold the ship fast, pulling up the fenders that protect its sides.

"Well, Parras. Good luck then. It looks," Polol

says with a smile, "like you're in good hands."
He throws Parras' backpack onto the deck of the
ship.

"Enjoy your hunting," Parras shouts. "And try
not to get into any trouble while I'm gone."

"That," the Skandar laughs, "I cannot do."

The captain goes to an ornate tiller and eases
the *Dark Sea* out of its berth, making an unusual
amount of engine noise as it slips into the
choppy water of the Inner Sea. The captain
shouts over to Parras, "Have you ever operated a
light sail winch?" Parras shakes his head. "No
matter. When I signal you, untie the light sail
and turn both handles; you see them there. You
must turn them together." He looks around,
then calls out, "Cylene, have you checked down
below?"

A scratchy speaker brings the answer. "Yes,
Father. Everything looks," a slight pause, "fine."

It would appear, Parras thinks, that this vessel
has not exactly been operating trouble free.

"I'm called Tolin," the man announces. "Now
get to your post and wait my signal."

Parras, feeling like a young boy once again in
class, runs to the winches. The sunlight glistens
on the water, causing him to squint. The steady
rocking of the small ship has him weaving back
and forth, thankful, for once, that his stomach is
empty. Then, he sees Tolin raise his arm and
drop it quickly. "Now!"

Parras unties the cord holding the shimmer-
ing light sail, and then he turns the winches,

©1986

moving his arms in opposite directions to roll the sail up.

"Together!" Tolin's voice barks out. "You must keep them even or the sail will not fill properly. Watch what you are doing! Cylene, is everything still fine with the meters?"

Again the speaker crackles to life. "Yes, Father, everything looks very good here."

Parras raises his eyes to the sail, its silvery material almost blinding in the light. Only halfway up, and already his arms feel the strain. Big droplets of sweat pop out on his forehead.

"Faster! We need the sail up now!" Tolin yells. And Parras redoubles his efforts, thinking only of that glorious moment when the sails will be completely unfurled and the winch will lock into place.

"Almost there!" Tolin yells. "Just a bit more. A little bit more." Parras' arms move steadily, in big circles, as if stirring twin pots of some giant stew.

"There! Cylene, the sails are ready."

And Parras backs away as the sails fill with the breeze and capture the sun's rays. He hears a series of funny clicks and popping noises, and then the ship seems to handle more smoothly.

Tolin comes walking over to him. "Well done. It's not that easy to get the sails up. Normally, I'd have Cylene do it, but it's better she watches the meters. This is, after all, an old ship."

And while Parras contemplates the image of Cylene raising the sail, an image that makes him

## Section 31

wipe the sweat off his brow with embarrassment, she comes up from below.

"Sorry for the quick departure. We don't have much time, but now we can talk. My father can run the ship till we get to Piliplok. My room is this way."

She turns and leads Parras to the fore section of the ship.

*Roll 3 D6.*

*If the total is the same or less than Parras' value for Wisdom, turn to section 26.*

*If the total is greater, turn to section 31.*

* **31** *

Parras follows Cylene down to her room, a tiny cubby that Parras guesses is at the very bow of the ship. Cylene sits down on a small wooden bench and gestures to Parras to sit on her bunk.

Cylene shuts the door behind them.

"It's best my father not hear us. He thinks we are merely engaged in a research trip for Valentine."

She uses the Coronal's name with a familiarity that startles Parras, and he wonders how and where she met him.

"My father is a good man, but can be somewhat overprotective. I must ask that you use your discretion when around him. I don't want him worried needlessly."

Cylene pushes her auburn hair off her forehead, and then pulls down a map off the shelf over her bunk. She lays it down next to Parras.

"When we arrive in Piliplok, I've arranged to join a caravan that will cross the river Steiche, right here," she says, pointing. "We'll leave the caravan at the river, and then proceed on foot to the reservation, here, in the North. With luck, that will take two, maybe three weeks."

"Not much time left," Parras offers. "Wouldn't a floater—"

"No," Cylene says sharply. "That would attract attention. Our only hope is to enter the reservation and find the Beliathys."

"And who is he?" Parras asks, annoyed that the leadership of this adventure is decidedly not in his hands.

"A Metamorph and," she adds quietly, a wistful look in her eyes, "a friend. He was a council leader for one of the local ruling organizations. He may be able to help."

"If he hasn't kidnapped Valentine's son himself," Parras says bitterly.

"With that attitude, we're sure to fail. I know the shapeshifters," she says sharply, "and my judgment regarding them must be trusted completely."

Well, thinks Parras. We're not exactly off to a good start.

## Section 32

*If Parras decides to rely on his Wisdom, turn to section 22.*

*If he decides to rely on his Intelligence, turn to section 25.*

*If he decides to rely on his Charisma, turn to section 28.*

\* **32** \*

Right, Parras thinks. Metamorphs are just great, no problem at all. Finest citizens of Majipoor. Except that maybe they want their planet back and some of them are willing to fight another war for it. And while Cylene is beautiful, stunning really, and obviously an authority on the shapeshifters, there are personal sympathies here that will bear watching.

*Turn to section 23.*

# ∗ **33** ∗

Parras smiles.

"Yes, Cylene, you are, after all, the expert. I'm really just along to help you in whatever way I can. My only interest is in finding Valentine's son, no matter what we have to do or who we have to befriend."

Or, he might add, who he would have to kill.

"Good. We'll get along much better that way." Cylene pauses a moment as she takes on a tentative look. "I was once involved with a shapeshifter. It was a professional relationship, until it changed, somehow. It left me very . . ." she searches for the word.

"Confused?" Parras guesses and she nods. "We've all felt that, Cylene, whether dealing with our race or another." She raises her eyes to him, and she lets a warm grin fill her face. "Yes, such is life in Majipoor with its many races. Now let me tell you what we must do."

Parras moves closer to her, smelling the tangy mixture of the wooden cabin and faint traces of her perfume.

*Turn to section 23.*

## * **34** *

"Your bunk is aft, under the main light sail. My father usually prepares a simple dinner about an hour before the sun sets. Tonight, I will start preparing you to enter the Metamorph Reservation.

"For now," Cylene says with an angry glare, "I'd like to be alone."

Parras gets up and, ducking his head to get out of the cabin, leaves the suddenly chilly room for the relative warmth of the empty passageway.

It will, he smiles to himself, be a long couple of weeks.

Parras makes his way to his cabin and opens the door. He is greeted by the startled squeak of an oversized rat, gray and plump. The rat seems to hover in the corner, to see just how rude this intruder might be. When Parras throws his pack onto the bunk a cloud of dust rises into the air, and the rat, sensing his eviction, departs.

The *Dark Sea* moves smoothly now, and Parras can just barely sense the motion of the small vessel as it crosses from crest to crest, traveling over the foamy whitecaps, staying well above the churning troughs of water below the hull.

His arms ache and, surprised, he lies down in

the bunk to rest for a few minutes before going topside to see if Tolin needs help. He thinks of Cylene, of Tolin, of Polol and, lastly, of Valentine. In the background he hears the soft whir of the ship. Before long, he is snoring loudly.

A sharp rap on his cabin door awakens him.

"There is some dinner, Parras. In my father's cabin," Cylene's voice awakens him brusquely.

"Be right there," he answers, for a moment completely confused as to his whereabouts. Am I on Zygnor, he thinks? Or perhaps I'm back on the Mount, sleeping off a belly full of wine? But no, he remembers, and hastens to fill his growling stomach.

He finds Tolin's spacious cabin and enters to see the captain and his daughter well advanced into the meal.

"We didn't wait," Tolin says, his teeth displaying some crusty bread not yet completely chewed. "Have a seat and begin eating. We don't go in for any niceties here."

There was some fresh meat on a wooden platter, perhaps some roasted mintun, and some succulent sliced dwikka. A steamy dish of some cooked grain was almost half gone.

Parras, feeling very hungry, fills his plate.

"My daughter says that you, too, are a scholar."

His mouth full, Parras nods.

"You know," Tolin continues, a sidelong glance at his daughter, "I don't trust my girl with those shapeshifters. Killed a few, I have, and they are the worst creatures you could ever fight. First they're one thing, then they're another. Drives you nearly batty when you are in a fight with them."

"Father," Cylene orders. "The Metamorph Wars are long over."

Tolin nods. "If you say so." Then, smiling wryly, he looks at Parras. "But I don't think they'll ever be over." He grabs the greasy, near empty platter of meat. "Some more?" he asks, and when Parras shakes his head, Tolin slides the scraps onto his own plate.

"Never like to waste food." he smiles.

Parras is scrubbing the rough ceramic plates, chipped and scratched from hundreds of simple meals, when Cylene comes up to him. "My father is on deck, smoking his pipe. I'd like to start your classes now."

"Classes?" Parras asks. "What do you mean, classes?"

"The history and biology of the Metamorphs." She leans forward to stare at the tub of sudsy plates. "After you're done here, of course."

Parras finishes the dishes and makes his way to Cylene's cabin. He knocks and she invites him in.

Her bunk is filled with books and maps, and she has arranged two chairs in front of it. "We'll do this a couple of times a day, Parras, until you can pass for an expert." She starts flipping through the books. "And that won't be hard considering the amount of ignorance about Metamorphs in our fair land."

And she talks, interrupted only occasionally by a question from Parras. She told the terrible saga of the Metamorph Wars, about the final burning out of the renegade bands in Alhanroel. She described the great migration of the shape-shifters to the reservation, a mammoth piece of land occupying almost half of the great continent of Zimroel. And she talked of the lingering sorrow of the Metamorphs, how this was once the great world of Piurivar, but they became prisoners of their own land. And her eyes light up describing the wonders of the lost city of the Metamorphs, Velalisier.

Parras' questions are perceptive, probing the exact sequence that led to modern-day Majipoor. He asks about the ruling council that runs the reservation as a separate country, and he asks for the history of the splinter groups eager once again to wage war.

And for the next two days, they meet frequently. Cylene is like a frantic professor, information gushing from her even as she piles books onto Parras' arms, books that he takes to his bunk and reads.

Gradually he comes to understand something that had previously been a few lines in a history book, some ancient lesson learned when he was a boy.

## Section 34

This, he thinks, was once their planet. We are no better than poachers, usurpers of what is not ours.

And with the realization comes the other, more sobering thought. It cannot be changed. What's been done has been done. The way of life on Majipoor is firmly set.

Cylene watches Parras' growing understanding with a sense of pride and wonder. She sees Parras not as merely another mindless soldier in service to the Coronal and Majipoor, but as someone capable of dealing with doubt and paradox. They were going over the map of the reservation when they felt the first bump.

"What's that?" Parras asks, a startled expression on his face.

"Come." Cylene smiles, taking his hand, warm now, Parras notices. "This you have to see."

She pulls Parras up the rough wooden plank steps. The sky is dotted with only a few clouds, but the brisk sea air is filled with the sounds of a most wondrous sort. Deep, gulping barks mix with high-pitched forlorn squeals. And everywhere they look, the sea is a foaming, churning, mass of sea-dragons.

"Aren't they wonderful?" Cylene asks.

Tolin is steering the ship through the herd, laughing and grinning. "There!" he shouts. "See that mother with her babies!"

Parras looks over and sees a big-bellied female, her long, trunk-like neck peering left and right, as if counting her young. Her head is a fierce, triangular wedge, but her eyes only register her concern for her young.

Her glistening fins are flared, creating an enormous wake that pushes the young dragons ahead of her. And all around, dragons of every age are moving south, toward the Great Sea.

"I've never seen anything like it," Parras says over the din.

"Migration season," shouts Tolin, obviously enjoying the frenzy of it all. "But I've never seen—"

He stops in mid-sentence. Cylene is the first to notice. "Father," she says seeing him standing stock-still. "Is anything—"

"Cylene, my energy thrower! Quickly!"

Already she is moving to a sturdy box near the entrance to the lower decks. Parras looks to her, then to Tolin, confused about what might be going on.

Sea-dragons, he knew, were generally gentle, harmless creatures. And Tolin seemed to be steering clear of them. What could . . .

Then he sees it. Coming from the outer circle of the herd, fins flapping angrily at the water, its enormous head chewing at the air even as it made a direct line for the *Dark Sea*.

Cylene runs up to Tolin and hands the energy thrower to him. "Why is it coming at us?" Parras yells. "What's wrong?"

Cylene comes running back. "Look at her

belly when she comes up," Cylene says, pointing to the charging dragon.

As the dragon rides each crest, kicking through the water, Parras sees the many teats, full and engorged.

"Someone took her babies," Cylene shouts over the sound of the dragons.

And Parras recalls hearing about dragon hunters who violated the laws protecting young dragons to supply the very rich with the tender, tasty delicacy of newborn dragon. Somehow, one of the big ships must have distracted or anesthetized this massive sea-dragon, and scooped up her babies.

Now any ship that came near her would be doomed.

Parras looks at Tolin taking aim with his energy thrower, all the time wishing that he could be the one to shoot.

"I've got her now," Tolin shouts. "Just a bit closer. Just a bit—"

The dragon dives under the water, and Tolin lowers his weapon.

"Now where could she be?" Tolin asks. Then, smiling, "Maybe she's thought better of it."

Parras is already running to Tolin, fearing the worst, when the dragon surfaces, its broad back pushing the small ship up, almost skewing its aft end into the churning sea. But Parras, gripping the handrail, takes no notice of that. He sees the energy thrower come flying out of Tolin's hand,

up into the sky. Too late, Parras thinks.

The ship slaps down in the water. Cylene looks to the light sails, flapping back and forth as they lose the wind.

The dragon rears up to bring its great body down upon the deck of the *Dark Sea*.

*If Parras kept his sword with him, turn to section 40.*

*If he handed his sword to Cylene, turn to section 35.*

## * 35 *

Instinctively, Parras gropes for his sword, only to discover, with a sickening feeling, that it's gone.

"My sword!" he yells, and Cylene, her eyes bright with terror, looks at him.

"Hurry!" she shouts, and Parras is already flying past her, down to her cabin. He kicks the door open and opens up the compartment over Cylene's bed. Then he hears a terrible sound, the side of the ship being smashed by the tremendous weight of the dragon. He wastes no time as he holds his sword ready to push the enraged sea-dragon back.

He reaches the deck and sees that the dragon has already severely damaged one of the sections of the hull. He raises his sword, ready to battle.

*The dragon has made its first attack. Turn to section 37.*

## * **36** *

Parras looks at Cylene's steely eyes, his hand unconsciously goes to the hilt of his sword.

"That, I am afraid, I cannot do. You might as well strip me naked. No, I'm afraid my sword must stay where I am."

Cylene shakes her head, her face flushed with anger. This, thinks Parras, is someone who is used to getting her own way.

"You don't understand, do you? *I* am the expert on the Metamorphs and, believe me, your carrying a sword endangers us both. They are highly suspicious creatures and, what's worse, they would waste no time in destroying an 'invader' of their reservation. You must leave your sword here."

Her hand, delicate but with finely etched veins that showed Cylene to be no stranger to hard work, reaches out to Parras.

## Section 37

*If Parras decides to give her his sword, turn to section 41.*

*If Parras still decides to keep it by his side, turn to section 38.*

* **37** *

Parras runs under the sea-dragon and brings back his vibrating sword. The dragon's great tail turns the water while its wings flap uselessly in the air. Then, it rises up, tilting its massive gray-green body first backward, then forward, and down, about to rip off a massive section of the hull.

THE SEA-DRAGON
*To hit the* Dark Sea: *10*    *To be hit: 13*    *Hit points: 14*
*Damage: (special—see below)*

*The sea-dragon will try to crush the ship enough times to sink it. Parras attacks first and if Parras hits the dragon, it will back off, stunned. It will then try another spot until the ship is sunk or it is killed.*

*If Parras hits the dragon with his vibrating sword, turn to section 39.*

*If Parras misses, and the dragon hits the ship, turn to section 44.*

*If they both miss, turn to section 42.*

## * **38** *

"No," Parras says quietly. "I must refuse."

Cylene moves to the door leading out of her cabin. "Very well. I have tried to explain. I hope you realize that our fate is now more in your hands than in mine."

Parras nods, not altogether displeased with that prospect.

*Turn to section 34.*

## * **39** *

Parras sends his great sword slicing through the leathery neck of the sea-dragon, and it screams out, a roar that fills the air. Parras' sword sends a yellowish ichor from the dragon's veins flying onto the deck, and his sword has rivulets of the fluid running down it.

"Again!" Tolin screams. "Before she can dive and surprise us somewhere else."

*Return to section 37 for the next round of battle with the sea-dragon.*

*If the sea-dragon has no hit points left, turn to section 45.*

## * **40** *

Thank heavens for my stubbornness, Parras thinks, as he pulls out his sword and runs over to where the dragon is rearing up, ready to crash down on the bow of the small vessel.

*Turn to section 37.*

## * **41** *

Parras considers Cylene's proposal. It might very well be dangerous to enter the reservation armed with a sword. It certainly would make it difficult for the Metamorphs to believe that they were, indeed, scholars.

Yet to travel defenselessly, through the wilds

of Zimroel, well, it went against everything he was trained to do.

He looks at her eyes, cold, unyielding—

(And something else! Parras thinks.)

"Very well. But if we should get into a situation that demands weapons, I'll do everything in my power to get some." He undoes the broad belt that holds his sword around his waist.

"The point," Cylene says matter-of-factly, as she takes his sword from him and sticks it into a compartment just above Parras' head, "is to avoid a confrontation." She closes the door to the hidden compartment, and the wood blends to make the alcove unnoticeable.

"True," Parras smiles. "But I've always liked being prepared for any eventuality."

Cylene opens the door, signaling Parras to leave.

*Turn to section 34.*

* **42** *

The ship tilts, sending Parras stumbling backward even as the sea-dragon plops down on the water, missing the ship completely.

"That was a close one, Parras," Tolin yells. "Go for the neck, and quickly."

Parras regains his footing and runs to the

side of the ship just in time to see the sea-dragon reappear.

"Hello," Parras says, looking right at it. "This time you won't be so lucky."

*Return to section 37 for another round of combat.*

*Return to section 37 for another round of combat.*

* **43** *

The sea-dragon rises up, almost out of the water now, flapping at the air before letting its great body come crashing down.

And when it does, it smashes the hull wide open.

The *Dark Sea* begins immediately to list, tilting down.

"She's gone!" Tolin shouts. "Try to get aft before—"

But the sea-dragon crashes down again, this time right on Tolin, and he's gone. Parras is holding on to the railing as the ship heels drastically, water up to the gunwales.

"Cylene!" Parras calls out. "Hold on and I'll try to get to you."

Parras crawls over to the other side of the ship and sees Cylene just barely holding on to a rope. Her feet are dangling right in the path of the dragon. "Parras," she cries out. "I can't hold on anymore."

"Hold on!" Parras yells, but even as he does so, the sea-dragon is over him, literally crawling its way up the sinking vessel. Its great head reaches down toward Cylene's legs and closes over them.

"No!" Parras screams, but the ship groans out its agony and slides into the churning sea. The sea-dragon's wings catch Parras as he slips down, protruding bony hooks digging into his side.

Parras yells as the seawater covers him.

*Turn to section 29.*

* **44** *

The ship bobs, its light sail flapping back and forth, losing most of its power. Parras takes a swing, but the ship heels, and he is thrown to the deck, just in time to see the great sea-dragon bring its body down on the ship's hull. The sound of splintering wood mixes with the slithering sound of the sea-dragon sliding off the deck for yet another attack.

*If the sea-dragon has hit the ship three times, turn to section 43.*

*If not, return to section 37 for the next round of battle.*

# * **45** *

Gurgling sounds burble from the many holes in the sea-dragon's throat. Its great, sad eyes, so much like a sea-going blave, blink and then close. All around the ship the other sea-dragons seem to clear away, mother dragons guiding their young, while the old bulls snort and turn sharply south.

"Well done, Parras. We could use the likes of you in Piliplok, aboard the dragon ships. Oh yes, the way you fought that thing at sea was—"

Cylene comes to the railing and gazes out at the herd, moving now in the distance. The dead sea-dragon floats nearby, its bloated body quickly filling with sea water. In moments, Cylene knows, it will sink to the bottom, providing a feast for the crusty-shelled arakas who will rip off great chunks of the meat and scurry under some cold, dark ledge. If the scent reaches them, giant papangos will plod their way down to the carcass and make short work of it.

"It's sad," Cylene says softly.

"What do you mean?" Tolin barks. "Sad that *we're* not taking the dive down there? Well, I much prefer being alive, Cylene, than feeding the claws of the arakas."

"No," she says looking out to the sea, as the

great hulk begins to bubble and sink. "Someone took her babies, sliced them up for the wealthy patrons in Ni-Moya. We just happened to show up."

Parras searches for a cloth on the deck, and finding one by the winches, he uses it to wipe his sword clean and then snaps the sword to his side.

The debate about his weapon, he hopes, is over. In fact, he'd like to get his hands on a small energy thrower, he tells himself. Just as soon—

"Parras," Cylene says. Parras looks over to her, beautiful and sad in the late afternoon light. "Thank you. We'd be dead now if it weren't for you." And then she moves quickly to go below deck.

Parras nods, feeling his adrenaline level slowly come back to normal.

How much more danger will they have to face, he wonders? Their task is so important, and yet an odd twist of fate could end their lives and, perhaps, bring about war to Majipoor.

"Well," Tolin says, clapping his hands together, "enough rest. We need to get the sails filled and look over the ship for any damage. And," he says, squinting at the sunlight, "I guess we have a few hours left to work. So, let's at it."

"Aye, aye," Parras laughs and puts an arm around the old man and gives him an affectionate hug.

They work well into the night, patching holes with a murky mixture made of the sap from the dwikka trees and the crumbled outer bark from the vramma tree. "It will hold till we reach Piliplok," Tolin says. Then, with a wink, "At least, I hope it will."

The sails fill once more and the *Dark Sea* stops its bobbing and dipping, as it travels a smooth, level highway made of the very tops of the foamy sea.

On his own, Parras scrubs the deck, trying to remove any traces of the day's battle. Only when he gets back to his cabin does he notice the sticky yellow stains spotting his pants and shirt.

He strips and throws his clothes in a corner.

And that night, he dreams.

It starts out soothing, a dream to take away the day's pain and struggle, and replace it with a kind of peace experienced maybe only a few times in one's life.

He was in the valley, well below the Mount, resting by the river Glayge near Amblemorn. At first, he is alone. There are some rich cheeses on a blanket, as well as some slices of juicy dwikka, and a bottle of dark thokka wine. In the dream, the rainy season has ended and now, before the valley bears the scars of the endless heat to come, everything is lush and beautiful.

He lies back and his heart seems at one with the beautiful world around him. The gentle smells and sounds of the river lull him.

And, in his dream, he shuts his eyes.

But, he hears a sound, the cracking of a small

twig perhaps, or someone's step on a pile of bunch fungus.

He sits up and sees Cylene coming toward him, dressed in a pale blue dress, her lustrous hair flowing, begging to be caressed. He hopes she comes closer. And she does.

Her mouth, so warm and open, moves, saying something to Parras. But, for some reason, he cannot hear it. He stands, eager to move closer to her, to wrap his arms tightly around her and pull her close.

"Cylene," he says, taking a step.

"Yes," she says, and then her tongue splits, becoming a pulpy red thing, slithering in and out of her mouth. The air takes on an acrid, displeasing smell as Cylene's hair turns into twisting, glistening tentacles.

"You're a Ghayrog!" Parras shouts.

Then, the Ghayrog is gone, replaced by some dark creature wielding an ax, something only to be seen on some fantastic entertainment cube.

He staggers back.

"Where is Cylene?" he shouts. "And Tylan, and Valentine?"

The creature changes again, and the Metamorph laughs. "Gone," it answers. "All of them except you."

"No," Parras screams, but he hears nothing coming from his mouth. *Cylene*, he calls, and again, *Cylene*. But he makes no sound.

Until he feels himself being touched by cool,

dry hands. He blinks awake and almost yelps in surprise when he sees Cylene sitting on his bunk next to him.

"Shh," she whispers. "It was just a dream."

Parras' eyes slowly focus and his breath begins to slow. "It was horrible," he says. "You were a Metamorph, and there was no one left, no one but me."

"It was just a sending from the King of Dreams," Cylene says. "Some twisted little joke that he uses to pass the time."

"Unless," Parras says quietly, "unless it came from the Isle of Sleep, and Our Lady. Then, it may be a warning about the future."

Cylene smiles, and puts a hand to Parras' forehead. "You're hot. I think that your dragon-slaying has taken its toll on you. Tomorrow you must stay in your bunk and rest. We have a big journey ahead. The day after that, we will reach Piliplok."

"Yes, perhaps you're right."

Cylene stands up, barely visible in the dark cabin. "I'm pleased to hear you were dreaming about me, Parras. I just hope your next dream has a more . . . pleasant outcome."

And then she was gone, leaving Parras to think of his dream, to think of Piliplok, and, just before falling asleep, to think of Cylene.

The next day is cloudy, and the air is uncomfortably cool. Tolin and Cylene spend their time working on the *Dark Sea*, oiling winches, neatly coiling the lines, and washing down the deck.

Parras offers to help but they seem to have the work so organized that he thinks a third person would only get in the way. And, Parras realizes, in some ways they now look at him differently.

He's the great slayer of sea-dragons. The savior of the *Dark Sea*. And once again, Parras feels that uncomfortable aloneness that comes from being recognized as a brave fighter, an expert swordsman, an effective killer. After all, he thinks ruefully, who wants to be close to a killer? You may need one from time to time. But when the bloodletting is over, it's best to show them the door.

With Valentine it had always been different. After the march on the Mount, Valentine had recognized Parras for his virtues as a fighter. But then he treated him as a person, almost a friend, and for a time Parras felt whole. Other people in court, including some of the ladies, continued to regard Parras as a glorified bodyguard. But Valentine's judgment seemed to stand, and, for most people, Parras became a person to respect. Someone with thoughts, and ideas, and passions.

In the quiet years that followed, Parras vented his need for a challenge in the rocky slopes of Alhanroel. And, when he was done with them, there'd be two other continents with mountains to climb.

Thus he knows some of the conflicting feelings going through Tolin and Cylene. Appreciation, yes, and respect. But also, quite near the surface, a bit of fear. So it has always been with the country's warriors. So it shall always be.

After sucking in the damp yet bracing air, Parras returns to his cabin to continue his studies. He is caught up now in the world of the shapeshifters, almost feeling that he understands them better than any of Valentine's advisors. And he wonders, too, whether it's dangerous to have so much sympathy for what everyone in the planet regards as a strange, antagonistic race.

The hours pass quickly and Parras arrives at dinner. Both Tolin and Cylene seem happy to see him, and they have a lively conversation about the city of Piliplok and its great harbor. When Parras goes to scrub the evening's plates, Tolin gently pushes him aside, saying that it must be his turn by now. And Cylene comes close to him.

"Another class?" he says, smiling.

Cylene shakes her head. "No class. Not anymore. You have absorbed more about the Metamorphs in these few days than most students do in a year of study. At this rate, you'll overtake me soon."

Parras smiles, pleased at the compliment. "I found them . . . interesting."

"I hope you still feel that way when we're in the reservation." She pauses, a tentative moment, and then she continues casually. "Would you like to talk some more on the deck? I think the clouds may have moved on."

Parras looks at her, surprised at the direct-
ness of her offer. "Yes," he says. "I'd like that."

Cylene grins at Parras and leads the way out,
up to the deck. Tolin sings some garbled ditty as
he scrubs the bowls and plates from the evening
meal.

Outside, it's dark and the cloud cover is still
firmly in place.

"Too bad," says Parras.

"Yes," says Cylene. "You see so many more
stars when you're at sea. So many places to
wonder about."

Parras leans on the rail, closer to Cylene, the
cool breeze dancing around them. "Surely
you've seen it many times? You're no stranger to
long sea voyages."

"It's something I never get tired of. I think
that if I could spend the rest of my life on a ship,
I'd be happy, really happy."

"You must have spent a lot of time on land,
studying with Metamorphs."

She goes quiet for a second, and then, "Yes.
Too much time. I lost my . . . judgment. I got
too close to my subjects."

"At least you had some judgment to lose,"
Parras laughs. "You should hear some of the
crazy stories told on the Mount about all the
races of Majipoor. No wonder the Pontifex re-
sides in the Labyrinth, away from it all."

Cylene turns toward Parras, a faint sheen of
moisture on her face. Parras looks at her. "Too

damp for you?" he asks. "There's a lot of spray slapping up in the air, perhaps—"

"I was wrong to judge you, Parras," Cylene says quietly. "I treated you like one of the ignorant ones, like—"

"Well," Parras laughs, interrupting, "I was. Until you educated me."

"No. Even before that, you didn't deserve my lack of respect. I know now why Valentine selected you to be with him as a friend." She pauses. "I, too, would want you as a friend."

"But I am," Parras says softly.

And then he feels Cylene against him, his taller body sheltering her from the wind and the dampness. He moves his arm around her to pull her even closer. She tilts her head up to him, a gentle, searching gesture. Parras leans down and kisses her.

A welcoming sound escapes from her lips, encouraging Parras to pull her tighter, to press harder against her eager mouth. Even in the murky darkness, her beautiful eyes sparkle.

He pulls back for a moment, holding her gaze, and together they consider how this moment will change their lives forever. And then they kiss again, wanting even more of each other.

"Oh, blast!" Tolin calls out, coming on the deck. "Still clouded over. Every time I get the autopilot working, there's nothing to see! Ah, I always enjoy it when the last night at sea is clear and star-lit. It's a good omen." Tolin digs out his pipe, oblivious to the activity he has just interrupted. "Reminds me of the time when I was doing some shipping for some wealthy merchants in Alaisor . . ."

Cylene smiles at Parras, a promise. "I have some notes to make tonight, and then I'm turning in. Good night, Father." She leaves the deck.

"Oh, good night, Cylene . . . Yes, where was I? Oh, Alaisor. Well, the sea had been filled with . . ."

But Parras isn't really listening. He thinks of Cylene, of the way her strong body felt close to him and how, he smiles, she didn't say good night to him, only her father.

A few respectable moments later and Parras excuses himself from the deck, pleading fatigue, leaving the old man and his memories to face the misty night alone. And he goes to Cylene's cabin and opens the door. A thin crack of light falls across her bunk and Parras sees her. She is naked and waiting for him.

"Well, I'm glad you escaped my father," she says lightly.

Parras unbuckles his swordbelt and quickly slips out of his clothes. "Only a fool wouldn't."

He goes to her, almost overwhelmed, and her arms pull him down to her.

"Slowly," she says. "It's been so long." Her legs wrap around his and pull him tight. And he tries to pace himself, to enjoy this moment. But then he too is lost in the wondrous pleasure of their two bodies.

# Section 45

"Now," she says quietly. "Oh, yes, now." And for the moment, they are perfect, whole, removed from the world. Finally, she relaxes her legs and arms.

"I didn't hurt you, did I?" she asks.

"No," he laughs. Then, quietly, "Should I stay or go?"

"Oh, please stay," she says eagerly.

And soon they fall asleep, curled together in the small bunk, with no dreams to disturb them.

"Piliplok!" Tolin shouts, pointing out the obvious. They are close to it, Parras notes, as he munches a crumbly biscuit from breakfast. "One of the jewels of Zimroel," Tolin continues. "A bit rough in spots, perhaps, but a great place for a good time. You will, of course, watch out for my daughter?"

"Rest assured, Captain. I will watch her as if she were my own," Parras says with a glance at Cylene.

Tolin goes to the tiller to navigate the *Dark Sea* to its prearranged berth.

"We're in the south end. Bit decrepit, but good enough for the old girl."

Once again Parras mans the light sails, hoping that bringing them down will be easier than raising them. Now Parras can make out the array of dragon ships, strange vessels with fierce carvings of sea-dragons adorning every part of the ship. The ships themselves are fierce killing machines, designed to quickly catch, kill, and butcher the dragons.

And Parras considers searching for the one vessel that happens to be dealing in young dragons.

Behind the docks, Parras can see the city of Piliplok itself, very old, but very organized, a planned city of eleven million inhabitants. Though the population is largely made up of Skandars, there are also many affluent Su-Suheris, who deal in luxurious items such as gems and fabrics, using the fine port to deal with all of Majipoor. Here too can be found the Pilgrim ships that sail for the Isle of Sleep on the first of every month.

"Get ready," Tolin calls out. Reluctantly, Parras grabs hold of the winches. "Now!"

And Parras turns them quickly, finding it just as difficult as the winches seem to pick up momentum which he struggles to restrain.

"Slowly," Tolin calls out. "Or you'll wreck them for the voyage home."

Using muscles that somehow must escape his regular exercise regimen, Parras struggles to ease the sails down until they neatly collapse onto the yardarm. Cylene comes out from below and begins strapping them tight, while Tolin guides the *Dark Sea* into her birth. Cylene runs to throw out the fenders to protect the ship. Seeing this great flurry of action, Parras feels more than a bit inadequate.

"What can I do?" he asks.

"I'll be jumping off. When I tell you to, throw me a line," Cylene answers.

Cylene waits until the ship gets close, and then she jumps onto the dock. "Now, the bow line," she calls. And Parras tosses over the vine-like line to Cylene. She calls for the spring lines, and soon the ship is tied up neatly.

Tolin throws a switch, and the engines go quiet.

"Well, I guess you'll be off," Tolin says. "Watch out, the two of you. Especially you," he says, looking at Parras, and for a moment Parras suspects Tolin perhaps knows who he really is. "I'll be here when you return, in about two or three weeks."

Cylene has a light pack prepared. She kisses her father on his grizzly beard and heads toward the city. Parras reaches out and shakes the old man's hand. Then Tolin turns away, going down below to putter with the innards of his precious ship.

Parras catches up to Cylene.

"Where do we meet the caravan?"

Cylene is walking briskly, taking big steps that force Parras to try and keep up.

"Piliplok is organized like a wheel, with some streets like spokes, and others, circles that go around them. The caravan is due to depart by this afternoon from an open park in the eastern part of the city. We should get there without any trouble."

They walk past the docks, now filled with just-returned dragon ships. Parras looks on in amazement, both at the sheer eccentricity of the ships' designs and the lethal efficiency they bring to their work.

Then he sees something that makes him stop. He grabs Cylene's arm. "Look," he says. And she turns to see the small, rust-colored dragon ship he is pointing out. She sees nothing out of the ordinary, and then, lying on the yellow stained deck, she sees the head of a baby sea-dragon, small and purplish.

"Practically a newborn," she says.

"I'm going down there to settle accounts," Parras says grimly.

"No," says Cylene. "If there's time we'll tell the authorities. But now, let's just get to the caravan."

*If Parras should decide to confront the dragon killers, turn to section 50.*

*If Parras should decide to keep moving on, turn to section 52.*

# * 46 *

Harbor authorities, all wearing expressions of varying degrees of confusion, fill the dock. Looking around, Parras realizes that corruption must fill this busy little harbor, and some of the people here most likely receive a good deal of money from illegal hunters.

They question Parras, their rudeness infuriating him, but he reminds himself that he must not let on that he is in service to the Coronal.

But the many gutted carcasses quickly provide evidences for Parras' claim and, after a warning to keep his weapon sheathed while in Piliplok, he and Cylene are allowed to continue.

"What's one ship among so many others?" Cylene asks, annoyed at his adventure. "The harbor, no, the whole city is a corrupt place."

"I wonder whether Valentine knows of this?" Parras asks.

"And I wonder whether we'll still be on time for our caravan?" Cylene asks more pointedly.

*Turn to section 52.*

## * **47** *

"Ah, here's a spot," Parras says, ignoring the lack of enthusiasm at his arrival. "You don't mind, do you?" he asks the Ghayrog.

In response, the Ghayrog turns his head away.

Cylene positions herself next to Parras and struggles to clear her mind.

"Are you headed to Bilfen, my friend?" he asks the Ghayrog. The Ghayrog shakes its head, sending its snake-like tendrils flying back and forth. "Thagobar, then?" Another shake. "Perhaps—"

The Ghayrog fixes Parras with a cold-eyed stare. "If you must know," he says, punctuating each phrase with a slither of its tongue, "I own a series of farms north of Velathys."

"Near the reservation?" Parras asks. "Isn't that a bit too close to—"

"It's fine. I get along fine with the shapeshifters and they get along fine with me. Not everyone, you see, is busy about other's business. Now, if you'll excuse me."

The Ghayrog gets up, and Parras takes a quick glance at Cylene who shakes her head.

No, not him, her eyes say.

Then Parras moves close to the Vroon. He is eating slowly, seemingly examining every piece of food as if it were some kind of biological specimen, bringing it up to his eyes, then passing it from one of his six arms to another, as if each hand must have the chunk before he dare eat it.

"Not to your liking?" Parras says good-naturedly. The Vroon ignores him. "I mean the food," Parras says. "You don't care for it? I have some salted bilantoon in my pack. If you—"

The Vroon looks at Parras, and, for a moment, Parras realizes his terrible mistake. If it is the Vroon who threatens them it will most assuredly be able to read Parras' thoughts. And that could be disastrous.

Parras starts to go flush in the face. Think of something, he tells himself. And he lets his mind picture Cylene aboard the *Dark Sea*, and then the terrible exciting sight of the migrating herd of sea-dragons. Anything but—

"Oh, excuse me," Cylene says, as her cup of juice tumbles onto the ground in front of the Vroon, splattering his legs.

"I'm sorry. So clumsy of me. I'm just such a hazard. Let me wipe it up."

The Vroon turns, distracted by Cylene, and Parras retreats. Another second, Parras realizes, and it would have discovered the truth.

"Nice talking with you," Parras says, casually getting up. "Coming, Cylene?"

"Yes," she says, still dabbing at the Vroon, whose eyes watch her dispassionately.

Parras tries to walk quickly, but without giving the appearance of hurrying.

"Nice save," he says. "I guess you knew what was happening." But Cylene is quiet, walking steadily to the wagon and their packs.

"It's him," she says softly. "He's on the caravan for only one purpose," she says.

"And what's that?" Parras asks, putting an arm around her shoulder and leaning down close to her.

"To kill us."

*If Parras and Cylene cannot be surprised by the Vroon, turn to section 59.*

* **48** *

*Roll 3 D6.*

*If the total is the same or less than Parras' value for Intelligence, turn to section 54.*

*If the total is greater, return to section 56 and select a place for Parras to sit.*

## * **49** *

"Mind if we join you?" Parras asks, setting his plate down on a rock between the Liimen and the Skandars. The Liimen look up in unison and shake their semicircular heads in a way that makes Parras dizzy just to look at them.

"Oh no, be our guest," the two young Skandars say, their bodies melted together as they pass the time dropping food into each other's mouth.

Cylene sits down quietly, knowing she must concentrate to pick up the source of the threat that she felt before.

"Where are you headed?" Parras asks the Liimen, bemused to be talking to such simple-minded folk. There is an awkward moment when they all try to answer until one says,

"Velathys," in a nasal accent. "Every year at harvest time we go." And at that the other Liimen all nod as if it were one of the most portentous facts in the universe. Parras continues talking about the harvest, and the farms they travel to, until he catches Cylene shaking her head.

No, her eyes say. Nothing here. Parras turns to the Skandars.

"And what about you two?"

They quickly withdraw their tongues from each other's maw. "Just married," the young female giggles. "Or can't you tell?"

The male extends his paw. "I'm Ferfen, and my bride's name is Silimat. We're going back to our village, at the foot of the Longhar Range."

And then, they smile at each other. Cylene shakes her head, barely hiding a grin.

The other travelers have finished eating and are searching for secluded places to spend the night.

Parras walks Cylene back to the wagon.

"No luck," he says matter-of-factly. "Maybe tomorrow we'll learn something."

Cylene grabs his hand and squeezes. "But the feeling grows, Parras. It *grows*."

Parras puts his arm around her and pulls her tight.

*Turn to section 59.*

## * **50** *

"I'm going down there," Parras says. And he takes the oddly shaped stones running down to the dock two and three at a time.

This dragon ship lacks the color of most of them, Parras notices. Obviously in need of a painting, the carvings on this ship have a dispirited air. Parras walks a narrow plank to get on board and finds himself standing next to part of a baby dragon carcass. As he stands there, a Ghayrog and a Human come on deck, standing close together, and Parras can sense their tension.

"Can we help you?" the Human asks.

"This," Parras says, kicking the dragon's head right in front of them, "is your work?"

The Human looks at the Ghayrog, his grin displaying a foul pit of a mouth. His speech is slurred.

"What if it is?"

"Killing the young is illegal," Parras says, taking a step forward. "And it nearly led to my getting killed by its mother."

They laugh. "Not too likely, mate. Not at all. You see," the Human says, lowering his voice, "we killed these little ones' mother. So, it must be another ship you are looking for." The laughter is loud now, and Cylene, watching from the stone walk above them, worries about Parras.

Parras remains unsmiling.

"Killing them is against the law, friends, and you can come with me and turn yourselves in."

The Human looks directly at Parras, taking the measure of him, and then nods at his companion.

"Sure, if that's what you want—" Then they both pull out long curved knives, tools of their trade, designed to fillet a dragon's skin with only the slightest effort. Sharp, and, in the hands of experts, extremely deadly.

DRAGON KILLERS
*To hit Parras: 11      To be hit: 10      Hit points: 6 each*
*Damage with knife: 1 D6−1*

*Conduct combat: The dragon hunters will fight to the death rather than face Piliplok's prison, where they have already been guests many times. If, after four rounds, Parras is still alive as well as one of the dragon killers, Cylene will have brought local harbor authorities to help Parras and stop the fight.*

*If Parras wins or it's the end of the fourth round, turn to section 46.*

*If the dragon killers win, turn to section 29.*

## ∗ **51** ∗

"Mind if we join you?" Parras directs the question to the Hjorts, since the Human seems lost to his plate of food. One of the Hjorts looks up and allows his head to grant a slight nod.

Cylene sits near Parras, trying to clear her mind, to see if she can read danger from any of these creatures.

# Section 51

"Headed to Velathys?" Parras says casually to the Hjorts.

One of the Hjorts, somewhat older Parras thinks, though it is hard to tell with their pebble-like skin, answers,

"No. Merely to Avendroyne. I work in the Hall of Records there."

"Yes," one of the others chimes in, "and we are in the Bureau of Taxes."

The Hjorts seem altogether pleased with themselves, although Avendroyne is not the most hospitable of cities. Parras continues talking to them, asking them about the supposed great wonders (it's a drab little place, Parras knows) and the serenity of the countryside (uninspired farmland, especially at this time of year). The Hjorts enjoy all the talk, but Parras notices Cylene shaking her head.

No, nothing here, her eyes say. Then, she gestures at the Human who, his meal finished, is getting up.

"And where are you off to?" Parras asks, standing.

The Human turns, his eyes dead, cold. Parras involuntarily takes a step back. "None of your affair, stranger."

Parras tries to keep a smile on his face. "Just curious about where my fellow travelers might be headed," Parras explains. He wants to keep talking to give Cylene the time to probe, to discover.

Is he the one?

## Section 51

"Some business in the interior, past the mountains?" Parras asks.

The Human gives Parras a slight smile. "Yes, in the interior, past the mountains. Now, if you will cease disturbing me."

The Human walks away.

"It's him, isn't it?" Parras asks excitedly when they're alone.

Cylene looks thoughtful, then shakes her head. "No. Though he has a secret, he doesn't pose a danger to us."

"A secret? What kind of secret?"

"I-I don't know," Cylene says. And Parras, looking right at her, knows that she's not telling the truth.

But for now, he doesn't press her.

"No luck," he says matter-of-factly. "Maybe tomorrow we'll learn something."

Cylene grabs his hand and squeezes. "But the feeling grows, Parras. It *grows*."

Parras puts his arm around her and pulls her tight.

*Turn to section 59.*

# * **52** *

As they move from the coastal area, the faint sea breeze fades. The warm season has begun and it leaves Piliplok's broad boulevards and narrow alleyways alike bathed in a blistering heat.

"This is not fun," Parras suggests. "Couldn't we hire someone to take us to this park? I'd be more than willing to part with a few crowns."

"As would I," Cylene says. "But if you want to pass as a scholar, then you must travel in a professorial way. On foot. And, we seem to have enough time to meet the caravan."

Parras smiles warmly, recognizing that his years on the Mount have, indeed, made him used to many luxuries. And, he reflects, an occasional season "roughing it" on a mountain-top can't change the fact that he has access to a floater at any time he wishes and, sigh, his own personal mineral tub.

Large enough for two, he thinks with a glance at Cylene.

So, they trudge up the grand Avenue of Lord Stiamot, one of Piliplok's five major boulevards. Legend has it that Stiamot made his triumphal return to Zimroel over the same route, back when it was a dirt and cobblestone path.

Now, all of Piliplok walks it. Sad-eyed Pilgrims biding their time until the next ship to the Isle of Sleep, and raucous Skandars wheeling and dealing in small cafes, and puffy-eyed Hjorts, who despite their authoritative demeanor seem to realize that they live on the periphery of life in Piliplok.

They pass shops offering a wondrous collection of prizes from all Majipoor, and beyond. Cylene pauses to glance at multicolored jewelry fashioned from minerals that change and grow, feeding on light much like a plant. And Parras admires a cluttered store selling weapons drawn from every place and period on Majipoor, from a simple knife to the latest, a most compact energy thrower.

Also along the route street vendors, many of them Liimen, are selling various grilled meats wrapped in a doughy blanket made out of glein. That, and a healthy juice made from lusavender, are Piliplok's specialties, and Parras and Cylene buy some to serve as their lunch.

Soon the great thoroughfare seems to lose its shops, and then its crowds, until it becomes again a simple stone path.

"There," says Cylene, pointing ahead. "Lord Stiamot's Park, and where we shall find our caravan."

They move briskly now, eager to be on their way, and eager, too, to be off their feet.

Parras sees them first, two large rotor wagons, each capable of holding six passengers and their luggage. As they get closer, they can see that both wagons look nearly loaded, ready to depart.

"Oh," Cylene says quietly. "I hope they saved our spaces."

A Ghayrog is standing beside the nearly full wagons, and Parras guesses that he must be in charge.

"Hello," Parras shouts, running over to him. "We have tickets for the caravan, to cross the River Steiche."

The Ghayrog responds by letting its tongue snake out and taste the air. "Yes. Two." He looks down at the list of names. "Two . . ." Then, looking up at Parras and Cylene, "Scholars. We are"—and again and again the tongue pokes out—"rather full. The woman is in that wagon," the Ghayrog says, pointing to the front wagon. "And you are in that one."

Parras shakes his head. "No. We want to be together."

"So be it," the Ghayrog says, the tendrils on his scalp twisting peevishly. "You may take the next caravan. Next week."

Cylene grabs Parras' arm. "It's okay, Parras. The wagons are close together. Besides, we have no choice."

"Prepare to leave," the Ghayrog orders to the drivers, both Skandars.

"You're right," Parras agrees. "Very well," to the Ghayrog, "we'll go."

"How wonderful!" the Ghayrog says with

leaden sarcasm. "Move quickly then. Everyone is eager to leave."

Parras leans forward and quickly gives Cylene a kiss. He doesn't like this, he thinks. There is dangerous territory ahead and he'd much rather be beside her.

"Let's go, young sir," the Skandar driver barks out. "As soon as we move, we can get a bit of a breeze."

Parras climbs onto the wagon. He sees the hitching post for the mounts, obviously not used since this wagon also has rotors to move it forward.

The Skandar eyes Parras carefully as he steps on, and Parras almost doesn't notice that she's a female, a great hulk of a thing with powerful arms. "My name is Pasti. My husband, Anitar, drives the other wagon. Here are the rules on our wagons."

Parras listens to her, and doesn't even realize the wagon is moving.

"No fights, no stealing, and no drunken stupors allowed. And, if you miss the caravan some morning, that's your problem."

Already the wagons are moving out of the park, smoothly gliding over the green-tufted hummocks, past dazzling patches of alabandina still in bloom, and over the small river that weaves through Piliplok. Parras sees Cylene's hair flowing in the wind and, even now, misses having her by his side.

"Your seat is in the back there," Pasti points,

and Parras steps over the other passengers. There is a Vroon, who already has his eyes closed and his six arms woven together—its traditional sleeping posture. There are two Hjorts, necks craning to catch every new object that pops into view. Male and female? Parras wonders. Possibly, but he could never tell. There is a Human also, whose blank expression makes Parras feel a bit creepy. And then, next to an empty seat, sits a female Ghayrog.

Parras excuses himself as he takes his seat. The Ghayrog nods, a few of its tendrils gently flopping on top of each other. The smell, Parras notices, is quite faint, thank heavens. Sometimes, especially when angry, a Ghayrog can give off an odor that can literally knock someone right over.

Glad to be sitting, Parras watches as the wagons leave the outlying reaches of Piliplok and follow a road leading east, into the heart of Zimroel.

And soon, Parras too is asleep.

"Parras. Parras! Wake up. You'll miss dinner."

Parras sits up sharply, once again struggling to recall just where he might be.

Cylene is in his wagon, gently pushing Parras' hair off his sweaty brow. "You need a shower."

Parras smiles at her. "I need dinner. I suppose we've stopped for the night?"

"Yes. I tried, by the way, to get someone to

change wagons so we could be together. But no one wants to move."

"Nice folk," Parras laughs. "An odd assortment of traveling companions."

Cylene's eyes grow dark. "There's something I have to tell you, Parras. I am here not only because I know the Metamorphs. Valentine selected me because I am a—"

"Psychic," Parras says quickly and Cylene's eyes widen. "Pretty easy to figure that one out."

But Cylene's eyes make Parras grow quiet.

"I've been getting this feeling about the caravan, a bad feeling, all day long. It started when I first stepped on and just kept growing—"

"Who's the feeling coming from?" Parras asks.

"That's the problem. I can't tell. It's as if someone is blocking me. But I sense danger to us here."

Parras sees his driver come walking up to him.

"Last call for some food," Pasti calls up at Cylene and Parras. The Skandar reaches up and pulls a rough-spun blanket from near her seat. "As for me, I'm gonna try and find a nice soft place to bed down with Alitar," she winks. "And I suggest you do the same."

Parras smiles, trying to erase the concern from his face. "Good idea." Then, turning to Cylene quickly, "As I said, I'm hungry."

He and Cylene walk away from the wagon,

## Section 53

out of hearing of Pasti, toward the other travelers, all squatting on rocks eating chunks of meat and vegetables. For the first time Parras sees the travelers in Cylene's wagon. Three Liimen, talking very animatedly to each other, an older Hjort who is sitting up with the two from Parras' wagon, and two young Skandars who spend much of their time cuddling and embracing, feeding each other clumps of food, and generally mooning about.

Which one is the threat, Parras thinks, which one?

"I'm gonna try to talk to some of our fellow travelers," Parras says quietly. "Sit near me and see if you can pick up anything from the conversation.

Cylene nods.

*Turn to section 56.*

\* **53** \*

*Roll 3 D6.*

*If the total is the same or less than Parras' value for Wisdom, turn to section 55.*

*If the total is greater, return to section 56 and have Parras select a place to sit.*

# * **54** *

If someone is interfering with Cylene's psychic ability, it must be someone with abilities equal to hers, Parras thinks.

And that is a scary thought.

That leaves out the Liimen for sure, and the Hjort. The Skandars certainly would be unlikely also.

Unless, of course, one of them is a Metamorph.

But Vroons are known for their telepathic powers. And the one in Parras' wagon has been anything but talkative.

*Return to section 56 and have Parras decide where to sit.*

## * **55** *

There are a few travelers that have Parras feeling more than a bit uneasy. That bland-faced Human, if that's what he is, definitely seems out of place. And the Ghayrog is certainly not a very talkative fellow.

Worst of all, the Vroon seems to be watching everything that's going on, and missing nothing.

*Return to section 56 and have Parras select a place to sit.*

## * **56** *

*See the chart on the page facing this one. These are the places that Parras and Cylene could sit down.*

*If they sit in area A, turn to section 49. If they sit in area B, turn to section 51. If they sit in area C, turn to section 47.*

*Before deciding, Parras can take a moment to rely on his Intelligence or his Wisdom.*

## Section 57

*If he should decide to rely on his Intelligence, turn to section 48.*

*If he should decide to rely on his Wisdom, turn to section 53.*

## * **57** *

Cylene stands up and the Vroon seems genuinely shocked. In a moment, Cylene senses what's happening. And she concentrates, blocking the flow of horror from the Vroon, calming Parras. Tiny droplets of sweat form on her brow, and she stares at the Vroon, whose eyes speak of age and power.

But no, Cylene says to herself. This won't happen.

And again—

This won't happen.

Parras' sword comes free.

The Vroon lets out a small gasp, stunned at the reversal.

"No," it mutters. "This cannot be."

"Oh yes," says Parras and he swings at the Vroon, aiming at the arm that holds one of the metal clubs aloft.

"Arrgh," the Vroon groans as, in an instant, the hand is severed from its wrist.

Parras brings the sword around for another blow.

"No," the Vroon pleads. "Please. No more."

"Then," Parras says quietly, "you will talk. Who sent you? What were you doing?"

An incredible agony fills the Vroon's eyes, and Cylene, her face pale and sickly after her tremendous effort, goes to the Vroon, takes the cloth bag and wraps it around the creature's wound.

"I was sent by the Metamorphs, by one named Glaan Cabalor. I was paid for my work, but I know nothing more."

Parras dangles his sword menacingly.

"And Valentine's son, Brynamir? What of him?"

"The Coronal's son? Please, I know nothing! Nothing at all. I am just—"

Parras raises his sword.

"No," Cylene says quietly. "He's telling you the truth. He's merely," she says with disgust, "an assassin."

They hear a gruff voice behind them, the sound of someone awakened from sleep. "What's going on here? We can't have this kind of—"

Alitar walks next to Parras and looks around at the strange scene.

"What have we here?" he says loudly. "A fight? We'll have no fighting in my caravan! No sir. I'm afraid that you'll have to—"

## Section 57

Parras quickly pulls the Skandar off to the side, to the shadows, even as a small crowd begins to build around them.

Cylene looks over to Parras and then sees the Skandar return. "You there," Alitar says to the Vroon, "walk to the wagon and I'll bandage your wound. And then I'll chain you to the wagon until we reach Avendroyne. Everyone else, back to sleep. It's all over."

The Skandar guides the Vroon away, even as the crowd, suspicious and a bit frightened, shuffles off.

"What did you tell him?" Cylene asks.

Parras puts an arm around her. "I merely told him that I was the Coronal's lieutenant and any help that he could give us would be greatly appreciated."

"But what if he tells someone?"

"Oh," Parras laughs, "I also told him that if he told a soul he would answer directly to Lord Valentine himself. I don't think we have to worry."

Parras and Cylene lie down together, their blankets covering them, and Parras strokes Cylene's hair. Soon he hears her rhythmic breathing, the gentle rise and fall of her chest, and he holds her tight as she sleeps, dreamlessly, in his arms.

*Turn to section 65.*

# * **58** *

Parras knows that it is just images, pictures sent to his mind. Like a sending from the King of Dreams.

But somehow that just doesn't help him. Soon all contact with reality will be gone, he knows, and what then?

A club smashing down on his head, or maybe something worse. He forces his dry lips open, knowing that there are only moments left.

"Cylene," he says, his voice a whisper. Then, louder, "Cylene. Help. Help!"

The metal spike is poised above Parras' head, while he stands there transfixed by the horrors of war.

"Cylene."

And then she moves, slowly, looking up.

*Turn to section 57.*

# * **59** *

Gradually the area around the wagons grows quiet, as each creature finds its own spot to lie down. This not being its sleeping season, the Ghayrog lingers by the fire, sipping cups of the thick, fruity, herb tea that was served with the cold supper.

But all around it there are the comforting sounds of creatures spreading out blankets, looking for clumps of moss to cushion their bodies, and having quiet conversations under a brilliant night sky.

Parras has just finished arranging their blankets alongside each other when he glances at Cylene and sees her looking straight up.

"You got your stars," he says gently.

"Yes. It's so beautiful here," Cylene says softly. "Sometimes I think I could be happy forever if I could live outside, away from cities, away from—"

"People? Ah, there I agree with you. Living on the Mount is like going to a party. There's not ten minutes each day when I'm alone, really alone. Sometimes, I just have to get away."

Cylene lies down on her blanket, putting her pack under her head. In the distance, she hears the other travelers, some still having quiet conversations, others already snoring. Parras comes beside her.

"Have you ever been off Majipoor?" Cylene asks.

"No," Parras laughs. "There's more than enough on this planet that I haven't seen."

"Sometimes I like to think that there's someone on another world somewhere thinking about my world, thinking about someone like me, at this very instant."

Parras puts his arm around her and pulls her close. Already, he can feel the night growing cool. "Well, if you get any messages, let me know."

And, as Parras rests his face in Cylene's hair, they fall asleep.

While all around them, the camp grows quiet, still.

*If Parras and Cylene cannot be surprised, turn to section 61.*

*Otherwise, turn to section 63.*

## * **60** *

The Vroon stands over them, heavy chunks of metal in a few of his hands, while one hand holds a heavy sack aloft.

Someone starts to stir, and the Vroon acts quickly. He brings one of the chunks down on Parras' head.

There, thinks the Vroon. That should take care of him for the time being.

He reaches down and scoops up Cylene, two hands firmly muffling her mouth, while the other powerful arms shove her into his sack.

Good, the Vroon thinks. It was almost too easy. Within a few days, he'll be in the reservation with his prize, and he'll be well rewarded too.

But the man seems to be moving again, just as the Vroon was about to give him another final, deadly blow.

*Turn to section 62.*

# * 61 *

Parras hears the steps, a mere shuffling in the dirt, and he knows he did the right thing by staying awake. But he lets him draw closer, not wanting to scare the attacker away before he can see who it is.

There, he thinks! He can almost hear the breathing, the struggling to keep the flow of air nice and smooth, restraining the fear it must feel.

Another moment, and it will be time to move.

Almost, Parras tells himself. Almost . . .

Now!

And Parras leaps to his feet and his hand goes to his sword. (And damn, he thinks, I wish I had an energy thrower!)

And the Vroon eyes him coldly, completely unstartled by Parras' sudden movement. In three of its arms the Vroon carries large metal bolts, like chunks of wagon axles. Another arm clutches some kind of sack. But it's not the arms that hold Parras' attention, it's the images that suddenly flood his mind.

Visions of horror. Towns burned to the ground, children grabbed from their mothers' arms and carried off to distant places, soldiers

## Section 62

bleeding, moaning long into the night until thankfully dying just before first light. Visions of war, sent by the Vroon to paralyze Parras.

And as the images grow more intense, Parras finds himself immobilized, frozen by the horrible mental assault directed at him.

*Roll 3 D6.*

*If the total is the same or less as Parras' value for Strength, turn to section 58.*

*If the total is greater, turn to section 60.*

* **62** *

Parras can taste the salty-sweet blood in his mouth. He opens his eyes and sees an odd sight.

It's a Vroon, standing like some floater mechanic, with tools and a sack of spare parts. What is he doing? Parras wonders. Perhaps Cylene will know—

He reaches over to touch her, to gently shake her awake. But there's no one there. And Parras knows what's happening.

The Vroon brings down a heavy metal spike aimed right at Parras.

VROON

*To hit Parras: 12     To be hit: 9     Hit points: 8*
*Damage done by metal club: 1 D6−2.*

*The Vroon has two attacks for every one of Parras'. It will place Cylene down while battling Parras. Parras has already received two hit points of damage.*

*If Parras wins, turn to section 64.*

*If Parras dies, turn to section 29.*

## \* **63** \*

It steps softly, this creature moving toward Parras and Cylene, taking care not to snap a brittle twig or crunch any leaves. And it moves right next to Parras and Cylene, so easy, it thinks.

Of course, it could kill them both. That would be simplest. But then, they'd never learn what Valentine knows. And that, of course, could be dangerous.

So, it's been told to knock out the man, kill him if necessary, and then take the girl, the girl with such a clear, strong power.

## Section 64

*Roll 3 D6.*

*If the total is the same or less than Parras' value for Wisdom, turn to section 61.*

*If the total is greater, turn to section 60.*

* **64** *

"So, it was the Vroon," Parras says quietly. "Perhaps I should have suspected him."

Cylene is close to him, shivering now in the damp night air.

"No, I should have known. The Vroon could easily block my powers. But you're hurt. Let me look at your wounds."

Soon a small crowd of the travelers have gathered around, led by a suspicious Alitar.

"Can you explain this?" he asks, one hand resting on his energy thrower. "A dead Vroon. Perhaps you forgot the rules? No fighting, my friend. None. I'm afraid I'll have to chain you to the wagon until—"

Parras stands up, his wounds bandaged but still oozing red. "A word, my friend, over here."

Reluctantly, the portly Skandar ambles into the shadows with Parras. A few moments pass, and they return.

"All right," Alitar announces to the other travelers. "Everyone back to sleep. We have a lot of traveling to do tomorrow."

The Skandar watches everyone melt away before calling his wife over to help him remove the surprisingly heavy Vroon carcass.

Cylene comes up to Parras.

"What did you tell him?" Cylene asks.

Parras puts an arm around her. "I merely told him that I was the Coronal's lieutenant and any help he would give us would be greatly appreciated."

"But what if he tells someone?"

"Oh," Parras laughs, "I also told him that if he told a soul he would answer directly to Lord Valentine himself. I don't think we have to worry."

Parras and Cylene lie down together, their blankets covering them, and Parras strokes Cylene's hair. Soon he hears her rhythmic breathing, the gentle rise and fall of her chest, and he holds her tight as she sleeps, dreamlessly, in his arms.

*Turn to section 65.*

# * **65** *

The morning starts early, with the Skandar
drivers preparing a light meal of fruit and tea.
No one mentions the Vroon chained to the front
wagon and, except for their somewhat bleary
eyes, everyone acts quite normally.

But Parras knows that the drivers will try to
go as fast as possible. If there's one assassin,
there's no reason to think that there couldn't be
more.

So the travelers eat quickly and the wagons
start moving into the fertile center of Zimroel.

The wagons hug the eastern spur of the Longhar Range, traveling the lower slopes, and below
them some of the richest land in Majipoor
passes by. Here there is rain and sun enough for
great, bountiful harvests that are the planet's
treasure.

Parras sees massive farmhouses, great estates
really, surrounded by endless acres of crops, all
maintained by an intricate hierarchy of farmers
and workers. In some places, it looks as though
the wagons have entered another country, with
its own rules and signs.

But it's off to the mountains, to the south, that
Parras looks. Climbing is such a direct, simple
challenge. The mountain is there, you must go

up. And then come down again.

Simple. Not like this.

With the expansive beauty of the continent rolling under them, the day moves fast. A midday meal is taken quickly, and before long, Parras finds that they have stopped for the night.

"Tomorrow we'll be at Avendroyne," Pasti says to Parras. "Then we'll unload that one," she grunts, pointing at the Vroon.

We must be higher up, Parras thinks, and the evening air is almost cold. He notices that Cylene doesn't eat much of her meal and she looks fatigued.

"You should go to sleep early tonight," he says, and Cylene nods, needing no convincing.

Later, while watching the Ghayrog stare into the fire, Parras hears Cylene stir. Then she calls out. A moan that speaks of some painful nightmare. He shakes her shoulder and calls her name—

"Cylene."

Then, she sleeps, quietly now, and whatever phantom was disturbing her is chased away.

By morning, Cylene looks her old self. Alitar has ordered the Human to switch wagons in order for Parras and Cylene to be together. Sitting side by side, they watch the wagons enter the city of Avendroyne.

Avendroyne marks the boundary of what is generally recognized as Metamorph territory. Though the actual reservation was still some distance ahead, Parras knows that from this point on the shapeshifters could be commonly seen. They do, in fact, freely enter the city, to trade their crops, to stroll the boulevards, and study the farmers who lived so differently from them.

The caravan avoids the main avenue, begrudgingly named Barjazid after the King of Dreams. People who depend upon the land for survival, Parras knows, want to appease any force that might threaten them. And the King of Dreams is well worth their respect.

They stop for a meal at a small cafe, and Pasti and Alitar escort the Vroon away, roughly holding the chains that keep its six arms tightly fastened to its body. The Ghayrog departs too, without a word to anyone, as do the Liimen who make up in effusiveness what they obviously lack in intelligence.

Alitar returns, and walks over to Parras.

"The authorities will want to speak to you. They say when you return this way will be fine."

"Thank you," Parras says, and seeing the Skandar makes him realize how much he misses Polol.

"Are you okay?" Cylene asks, noting Parras' faraway look, and Parras smiles.

"Yes. I'm just missing someone, a friend."

For a second, Cylene's face adopts a hurt expression.

"No," Parras laughs, "not *that* kind of friend."

"Let's go," Pasti yells. "We must be at the River Steiche by nightfall. Load up."

Cylene smiles, stands, and pulls Parras up. "Good," she says. They run over to the first wagon and, waiting a moment for the Hjorts to lumber on, the wagons set off.

The wilderness begins quickly, as if somehow the caravan had taken a wrong turn. In the distance, Parras sees the dark foliage of the jungle, where dazzling fire-shower trees alternate with the broad-leafed vrammas. And everywhere there are flowers in bloom, a dizzying array of color and scent that has all the travelers' nostrils twitching.

But it is when they begin their descent to the river, scattering flocks of roosting spinner birds and startling the toothy dhiims who excitedly glide from one branch to another, that they leave the world behind.

It's a chilling feeling, Parras thinks, to know that soon they will be on foot here, alone. With just the vibration sword and some dried pack food to keep them company. The caravans will head north in the morning, to Ilirivoyne.

The river is a strip of white water, its constant roar fills their ears even when they are still far away.

Alitar stops his wagon. "We'll camp here," he announces. "But everyone stay close. There are dangerous things in these parts."

Dangerous?

To be sure, Parras agrees, and he and Cylene set their blankets up quite near the wagons for this night.

## Section 65

Dangerous things.

There are the Metamorphs, of course. Perhaps not dangerous but certainly unpredictable. And there's the mouthplants, absolutely deadly if you should wander into a patch. And while geography was his weak point, Parras is pretty sure that the Forest Brethren, with their nasty blow guns, often hunted in just this area. It gave Parras little encouragement to see Pasti and Alitar walking around with their energy throwers close to their side.

The evening meal, though, was fresh, with some food picked up in Avendroyne. And, with the Vroon and the Ghayrog gone, a convivial atmosphere settled over the travelers, as each told a humorous story of some other trip, or some other adventure.

The talking went on well into the night as if everyone were reluctant to finally go to sleep to face the darkness alone.

But early morning found everyone huddled close together and Pasti had to raise her voice to get the sleepy travelers moving. "We're off now. Let's go, everyone. A quick bite, then on to Ilirivoyne!"

Cylene and Parras stand up and watch the others prepare to leave. Pasti walks over to them. "You're sure you want to go on with this . . . Whatever it is you're doing? We could still take you with us."

Cylene gives the shaggy driver a hug. "No. Thank you. We have to go into the reservation, through the pass to the south."

"And believe me," Parras smiles, "we'd like nothing better than to go with you."

Alitar walks over, holding a steaming mug of tea. "Still not coming? I don't know what you two are up to. Craziness, it seems like. But," he says, putting an arm around his wife, "we wish you good luck."

"And," Pasti says, one arm reaching to her side, "I want you to take this." She hands Parras her energy thrower.

"No," Parras says as he looks at Cylene. "I mean, I don't think we can—"

"Just till you reach the reservation then." Pasti says. "If you run into some of the Forest Brethren your sword won't do you much good. After that, just bury it. You can recover it later."

Parras smiles. "I—"

"Thank you," Cylene says, taking the weapon. "One way or the other, we'll see you get it back." She straps on the energy thrower.

"Well," Alitar says, grinning, "we're off." He hugs Cylene and Parras together, his arms encircling them like some great shaggy rug. Then Pasti gives them a squeeze. "Come back," she whispers, "alive."

The drivers board the wagons, and waving their arms, they leave, the sound of the wagons drowned out by the constant hiss of the nearby water.

For a moment they stand there. Looking at the wagons, feeling like young children watch-

# Section 65

ing their parents leave on a long trip. Then Cylene takes Parras' hand and pulls him south, toward the pass.

"I believe," she says lightly, "that there is some climbing involved. Think you can handle it?"

"Perhaps," Parras laughs. "Perhaps."

They try to pace themselves, moving briskly, but pausing frequently to rest. By nightfall they reach the entrance to the pass, a narrow gorge that runs parallel to a small stream. To the west is the Velathys Scarp, and to the south, Parras knows, is the Metamorph Reservation.

They sleep huddled together, cold now on the high ground. And they dream together . . .

It's a city. An enormous crystal city of endless spires and arches. In the light, it dazzles their eyes with an almost unwatchable beauty. At night, it shines with a jewel-like intensity.

They are inside it, together, before a creature in a long, blood-red robe.

It is a Ghayrog. And it seems to ignore them as its attendants flutter about, adjusting the robe, fixing a crown.

Then it looks at them, its tongue flicks out toward them, long, longer, longer still until it touches their faces with a slimy lick.

Then the robe begins to spread, as if it were melting, and the redness is everywhere, filling the great hall, moving toward their feet, creeping up their legs.

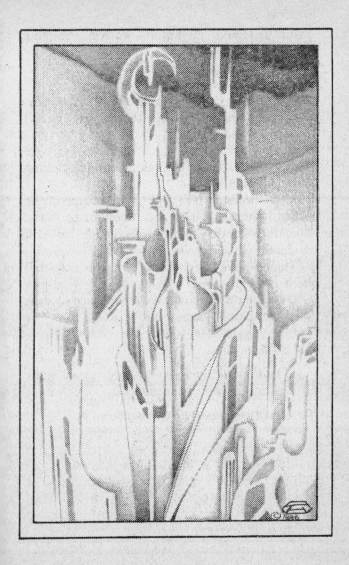

## Section 65

But the red is liquid, flowing, moving everywhere—

They clutch each other tightly.

(As they do in their sleep.)

The redness rises, covering their bodies, covering their mouths, until, they know, it will cover all of Majipoor.

They awaken.

(Sweaty now, their clothes damp and sticking to their bodies.)

Parras holds Cylene tight. "I'm scared," he says quietly. "This is all too much for us to do. What does this dream mean? And if it's war, or if it's death, what can we do to stop it?"

Cylene kisses his cheek, and Parras sees that she is crying.

"One person can make a war," she says softly. "And one person can stop it."

*Roll 3 D6.*

*If the total is the same or less than Parras' value for Intelligence, turn to section 72.*

*If the total is greater, turn to section 70.*

©1986

## * **66** *

Parras is able to get his vibration sword out and ready to strike. He looks around for a good place to slice the tendril in two.

*Roll 3 D6.*

*Parras can hit the plant on a roll of 14 or less, slicing it in two. If he does so, turn to section 76.*

*If he misses, turn to section 71.*

## * **67** *

They begin moving at first light, feeling cramped and achy from their cold night's sleep.

"I assume you know where to take us?" Parras asks "This isn't one of the official entrances to the reservation."

"If we tried coming in through the normal route, we'd never reach Beliathys and the Council," Cylene says. "Everyone is turned away. With luck, this should take us to the road that runs right through the center of the reservation."

Parras stops and taps her shoulder.

"And that may not be so wonderful. Look." Cylene follows Parras' gaze.

"Oh, no," she moans.

It's a small village, a few shacks really, and a small plot of land. Burnt to the ground, and still smoldering.

"Maybe two days old," Parras says grimly. They walk close to it, the wind thoughtfully blowing in the other direction. "Parras," Cylene says quietly. "Look. Over there." And all around the blackened foundation of the small building are dark, curled up shapes.

"People," he says. "So much for the peaceful Metamorphs."

"But," Cylene says angrily, "you don't *know* it was them. It could have been—"

"Who?"

Cylene stops. "I don't know. Maybe someone who wants this war."

"Or maybe it was just the Metamorphs . . . How about passing me the energy thrower?"

"Is that all you've learned?" she says sarcastically. "When confused, reach for a gun?"

"It served me well in the past." They walk away, silently now, each nurturing their own fear. The path narrows to a simple trail, and then, at times, the trail threatens to disappear completely.

They pass a large pond, its surface covered with bright yellow flowers. Off to the corner Parras sees a giant gromwark resting on the shore, its two front sucker feet flopped on a moss-covered log. It watches them without interest."

"Can we stop here?" Cylene asks. "A few minutes' rest wouldn't hurt."

"Certainly," Parras answers. "Be my guest." And he throws his own pack against a tree stump and attempts to shut his eyes. Cylene finds some other spot away from him.

He doesn't like snapping at Cylene. But her faith in the Metamorphs is just so incredibly exasperating. It was easy to be understanding while reading about them on the *Dark Sea*. But here, inside their territory . . . Well, that's another story.

Then, feeling the lack of sleep from the night before, Parras lets his eyes close.

Parras awakens to the sound of screaming.

The voice echoes eerily through the leafy corridors of the jungle, a disembodied sound. Parras looks around and calls out,

"Cylene."

Then, the scream is more desperate and Parras knows that something terrible is happening. He listens for the direction of the sound and then runs, jumping over great twisted roots and dodging the curling vines that dangle from the trees.

At first the sound seems to grow fainter, and he groans, knowing that he's gone in the wrong direction.

So he runs another way and the voice, Cylene's voice, is stronger now, even as it is mixed with a pitiful crying.

He calls to her, trying to let her know that help is coming, even as he imagines some of the horrible things that might be happening to her. Perhaps, he thinks, she has been attacked by Forest Brethren. Or maybe some wild animal has her cornered.

He runs harder, and the sweat flies off him as he pushes his way through the jungle.

Then he sees her.

She is sprawled on the ground, her hands drained white as they clutch an exposed root. While around her two feet are wrapped the thick rubbery tendrils of a mouthplant.

But Parras has to stop. To just run in there, to try and pull her out, would foolishly risk becoming trapped himself. Behind Cylene he can see the foot-wide opening of the plant, a great cup lined with hungry-looking organs quivering in anticipation, and a greenish fluid that can dissolve metal.

Her fingers are slipping, Parras can see.

"Please," Cylene begs, "help me."

Parras checks the jungle floor around her, scanning for any other vine-like tendrils that could whip around his legs, and pull him away before he could save Cylene.

It appears clear, except Parras knows that the plant's hunter-tendrils, extending many feet in different directions, are often under the ground,

## Section 68

waiting for some tell-tale movement on the dirt.

He sees her fingers begin to slip and her body slowly slide in the direction of the plant. And he knows he can't wait any longer.

He runs to Cylene.

And he is almost next to her when a tendril snaps out of the ground and whips around his neck.

"Ah," he gasps, as it quickly closes around his throat and begins to squeeze.

*Roll 3 D6.*

*If the total is the same or less than Parras' value for Dexterity, turn to section 66.*

*If the total is greater, turn to section 68.*


* **68** *

Parras reaches for his sword, but the plant's tendril snaps him around, and he falls to the ground.

*Roll 3 D6.*

*If the total is the same or less than Parras' value for Constitution, turn to section 73.*

*If the total is greater, turn to section 75.*

## \* **69** \*

"Keep walking," Parras says quietly. "We'll just pretend that we didn't hear him."

"That's far enough," the Metamorph announces.

Parras hears other voices behind them, three, maybe four.

"Well," he says, whispering to Cylene, "I guess that didn't work."

*If Parras should decide to stop and talk with the Metamorphs, turn to section 74.*

*If Parras should decide to go for his sword, turn to section 77.*

## * **70** *

"Such a confusing dream," Parras says. "We're heading for the Metamorph Reservation and we dream of Ghayrogs."

"More tricks from the King of Dreams," Cylene suggests.

"Perhaps," Parras says. "Perhaps."

*Turn to section 67.*

## * **71** *

Parras brings his sword down, but the hunter-tendril of the mouthplant gives him a sudden jerk, and he goes sprawling to the ground.

The thick tendril begins tightening around his neck.

*Roll 3 D6.*

*If the total is the same or less than Parras' value for Constitution, turn to section 79.*

*If the total is greater, turn to section 75.*

## * **72** *

"It's Dulorn," Parras says quietly.

"What?" Cylene asks, starting now to shiver.

"The city. I've seen it before. A crystal wonder. The Ghayrog city of Dulorn."

"But if the dream is a Sending," Cylene asks, "why would we dream of Dulorn and Ghayrogs?"

"Why, indeed?" Parras says.

*Turn to section 67.*

## *- **73** *

The hunter-tendril tries to tighten around Parras' throat, and he knows he may only be able to make one swing of his sword.

He reaches down and pulls his sword free.

*Roll 3 D6.*

*Parras will hit the tendril on a total of 12 or less on 3 D6. If he does so, turn to section 76.*

*If not, turn to section 71.*

# * **74** *

"Why?" asks Parras, feeling it advisable to stop and talk to the shapeshifter. "We just happen to be scholars on our way—"

But the shapeshifter has raised an arm and they are suddenly surrounded by Metamorphs, some holding oddly decorated spears, while a few hold their finely carved dirks pointed directly at Parras and Cylene.

"Hand over your weapon," the leader of the group demands.

Parras looks around and wonders just what the intelligent thing to do might be.

Then the Metamorph's body seems to pulsate and ripple, and Parras stares in horror as he sees it become a mere image of himself, saying again,

"Hand over your weapon."

The group of shapeshifters seems to stir uneasily. The Metamorph changes again, and now there are two Cylenes, absolutely identical, Parras notes with fascination.

"Please, Parras," one says, and Parras wishes that Polol was here. Somehow these kind of things just didn't happen when the Skandar was in tow.

"Very well," Parras says, undoing the buckle

and handing the sword to the Metamorph, who once again returned to its natural form.

"Now," the leader of the group says, "you will follow us."

"Where are we going?" asks Parras. "Where are you taking us?"

"To the Council," the Metamorph says evenly. Then with a glance at Cylene, "To Beliathys."

*Turn to section 80.*

## * **75** *

Parras feels himself start to black out. He needs air and he needs to cut the tendril now!

Cylene's screams fill his ears.

*If this is the first time Parras has been at this section, turn to section 79.*

*If Parras has been at this section before, turn to section 78.*

## * **76** *

Parras cuts the plant with a quick slash downward, and the tendril loosens around his neck. Suddenly, Cylene cries out, panic-stricken.

The plant has pulled her loose and is dragging her over the ground.

Parras runs to her now, ignoring the possibilities of other tendrils that might rise up, ignoring the hungry sounds coming from within the mouthplant.

Cylene is sliding now, her fingernails digging into the dirt to try and slow the relentless pulling of the plant. Parras jumps in her path.

"The hell you will!" he screams, and he brings down his sword, slicing the tendril in two. One parts snaps back to the plant, while the other loosens its hold on Cylene's ankles.

"Doing a little private botany work?" Parras asks. "I should have told you that the mouthplants are especially hungry at this time of year."

Cylene takes his offered hand and pulls herself up.

"Thank you," she says quietly. "I know about the filthy things. I guess I just wasn't thinking."

"Anger can do that," Parras says quietly.

Cylene looks at him and gives him a broad

smile. "And how should I reward my savior?"

"There are," Parras says, grinning, "a number of traditional ways."

Cylene comes close to him, pressing against him. "I think," she says quietly, "I know one that will do fine."

And they walk back to their camp and make love, as the singing ferns fill the afternoon air with an eerie harmony and an occasional gihorna calls out as it flies overhead.

They take their time, exploring each other's bodies, forgetting, for the moment, where they are and what they are doing, until, exhausted, they lie together on their backs, looking at the dense roof of leaves overhead.

"We must start," Parras says reluctantly.

"Yes," says Cylene, standing up and stretching, her body still sweating and dappled by blotches of sunlight. "Perhaps it will be cooler traveling in the afternoon."

So they begin moving once more into the very heart of the Metamorph Reservation. At some spots, it seems as if the jungle had been cut back, perhaps for a small farm, and then abandoned. The shapeshifters, Parras knows, tended to use the jungle as a barrier, sealing off their world from that of the many races of interlopers. They were shy, some said. Secretive, certainly. Hostile, according to most.

Then they see their first shapeshifter on the next day, just after setting out. It is impossible for them to tell its age or sex as it stands there, in a small clearing, watching them with eyes that tell no story.

"Hello," Parras calls, even as he examines the creature. It's much taller than a Human, he notices, and fragile-looking. It's the skin, though, that Parras finds most fascinating. Its pale, almost translucent quality makes it look as though it has no skin at all. And the eyes, sloping down into dark sockets, seem expressionless. The Metamorph's hair, green, rubbery-looking, hangs limply off its head.

"Hello," Parras says again, but the Metamorph runs away.

"Is that a good sign or a bad sign?" he says to Cylene.

"Who knows?" she says with a bemused expression. "At least they'll know we're here. I just hope we can get to the road. The main city, more of a town really, should be just a little east of here."

Later, they see two more Metamorphs, identical, each wearing a skimpy cloth around their waist and the small dirk that is the shapeshifters' favorite weapon. Parras calls out to them, but they too dart away.

It's late afternoon when they reach the road. The jungle seems to stop, ending in a series of small farms on either side of a wide dirt path.

"There it is!" Cylene says. "We didn't have far to go, Parras."

A shapeshifter farmer comes out of his house and stares at them as they walk through one of his fields. He watches them, and is eventually joined by another (A female? Parras wonders) and then three smaller Metamorphs.

"We must be an odd sight for these parts," he says.

"Definitely," Cylene agrees. "When I was here years ago I always had them looking at me. You grew to know what it feels like to be an alien. I was the monstrosity. I was the—"

They reach the road, and Parras touches Cylene's arm. A Metamorph is standing there, looking at them impassively, apparently waiting for them.

"Just keep walking," Cylene says quietly.

They approach the Metamorph, smiling and trying to act as if they have every right to be here.

"Stop," it says in a surprisingly deep, resonant voice. "You must stop."

*If Parras should decide to keep walking, ignoring the Metamorph, turn to section 69.*

*If Parras should decide to stop and listen to the Metamorph, turn to section 74.*

*If Parras should go for his sword, turn to section 77.*

# * **77** *

Parras goes for his sword, quickly raising it and turning to face the Metamorph.

"No," Cylene calls to him.

And then they are surrounded by Metamorphs, a half dozen or more, some armed with long spears, a few with their dirks held pointed at Parras and Cylene.

"Put down your weapon," one of the shapeshifters says, and then, as if eager to confuse Parras, it changes, its body somehow stretching, going blurry, until Parras faces a mirror image of himself, saying, "Put down your weapon, Parras."

"Do it," Cylene says quietly.

"We are scholars," Parras says goodnaturedly. "Here to study—"

Then the creature changes again, its body growing smaller, and Parras faces two Cylenes, each encouraging him to lay down his sword.

"Last chance," the Metamorph-as-Cylene says. "Then, these Piurivars will kill you. You are, after all, trespassing."

Would that Polol was here, thinks Parras. Somehow things like this never happened with the Skandar in tow. He lets his sword fall, and a shapeshifter quickly gathers it up, while another takes Cylene's energy thrower.

"Now," the leader of the group says, "you will follow us."

"Where are we going?" asks Parras. "Where are you taking us?"

"To the Council," the Metamorph says evenly. Then, with a glance at Cylene, "To Beliathys."

*Turn to section 80.*


* **78** *


Parras' hand tightens around the hilt of his sword, and he starts to bring it up hoping that he can stay conscious for just a few more seconds.

But then the tendril seems to contract even tighter, and Parras knows it is hopeless, as the sword falls from his hand.

*Turn to section 29.*

## * **79** *

Despite the plant squeezing tighter, Parras is able to stand and bring his sword around for a swing.

*Roll 3 D6.*

*Parras will hit the plant's tendril on a roll of 12 or less on 3 D6.*

*If he does so, turn to section 76.*

*If Parras misses, turn to section 71.*

## * **80** *

They walk, drawing glances from Metamorphs standing in the fields, and young Metamorphs climbing trees, their slender six-fingered hand clutching a branch as they gape at Parras and Cylene.

At first they head east, and then, unexpectedly, they veer off the road and begin climbing a weaving trail that seems to wander lazily up the hill.

And all the time that they walk, Parras holds Cylene's hand tightly, giving her a reassuring smile, trying to tell her that everything will be okay.

When, in fact, he didn't really have the slightest idea how all of this would turn out.

They climb, and then the hill begins to flatten, until it leads to a depression and Parras feels, now more than ever, the alien nature of the Metamorphs.

He sees what at first looks like an immense oval of oddly shaped stones. Most of them appear to be twelve feet long or more, cut at random angles, making them all seem to be some oversized geometric play set.

"What is it?" Cylene asks quietly.

One of the Metamorphs glances over as if to rebuke her for talking.

"You've never seen anything like this before?" Parras asks. "When—"

"No talking," one of the Metamorphs orders.

They reach the depression and, after depositing Parras and Cylene at its center, surrounded by the stones, the Metamorph guards withdraw.

A horn blows, a strange, primeval sound that echoes crazily off the stones. Then, from different parts of the oval, other shapeshifters appear, advancing steadily toward Parras and Cylene. And, as they walk, they change.

©1986

Dizzily, they twist and turn their bodies, nearing first Parras and then Cylene. They shift again, becoming now a Ghayrog, now a Hjort, now a Vroon.

"What are they doing?" Cylene asks nervously. But Parras is too fascinated watching to even attempt an answer.

The Metamorphs form a circle around them, slowly letting their bodies return to their normal state.

"We are Piurivars," one states. "And this council is in session.

Again, a horn blows, a chilling, strident sound that seems to come from nowhere and everywhere at once.

"You stand accused of entering the reservation illegally and trespassing. Before we decide your fate, do you have anything to say in defense of your actions?"

The Metamorph's eyes are passive, dull, dark pools that rove over Parras and Cylene with an icy detachment.

"Is one of them Beliathys?" Parras asks Cylene.

"I . . . I don't know. One of them could be. I cannot tell."

Parras looks at her, confused, uncomprehending. "You can't tell? You mean, you can't remember?"

"No. It's—"

But Parras turns to the circle of Metamorphs and calls out, "Beliathys!"

## Section 80

And one of the Metamorphs seems to register surprise and then steps forward.

"I am Beliathys."

And Cylene puts a hand to her mouth and whispers, "Beliathys?"

The Metamorph comes closer, and with each step he shifts, gradually adopting human features. A dark, handsome face form, and lively blue eyes, and, at last, a half-smile.

Cylene looks at him. "Beliathys," she says firmly.

"It is a serious thing you have done, Cylene," he says, "bringing this stranger inside the reservation. And I am merely one of the Council."

"Let us decide their fate," another Metamorph calls out. And Beliathys withdraws, resuming his natural shape.

"They must be locked away, lest other interlopers decide to invade our land. They must not be allowed to go free."

The Metamorphs nod, and then discuss the matter with each other.

"Parras," Cylene says sharply, "we have to do something."

"Agreed," says Parras. "But what shall we do?"

One of the Metamorphs is signaling to their erstwhile guards.

*Turn to section 90.*

## * **81** *

"We've got to get out of here," Parras says to Cylene. He grabs her hand and begins pulling her away.

"Stop!" Beliathys calls, but Parras is intent on moving as fast as he can, down the slope.

"Faster!" he yells at Cylene.

But then one of the spears comes flying through the air, a graceful arc that sends it plunging into Parras' back.

He stops, an odd pain coming from somewhere behind him. Cylene cries out to him,

"Parras!"

*Turn to section 29.*

## * **82** *

"Try to distract them," Cylene says. "I will see if there are any here who know of Valentine's son."

Cylene begins looking at the Council members even as she blocks out Parras as he speaks to them.

## Section 82

One by one, as she studies them, Cylene reads only fear and confusion. They obviously regard Parras and Cylene as threats. Then she comes to one Metamorph, near the far corner of the jumbled stones that make up the meeting place, and she sees something different.

She sees him in a great hall, surrounded by Ghayrogs. They are laughing and talking, sipping from great silvery goblets of wine. While before them stands the small, fair-haired son of Valentine.

But it's the city that she sees most clearly. The glimmering, crystal city of the dream she shared with Parras.

That city is where Brynamir is being held, Cylene knows, and that Metamorph is one who knows about it. Then, with a sudden tightening of her stomach, Cylene realizes something more.

This shapeshifter is also the one who sent the assassin against them.

*Turn to section 94.*

## * **83** *

"We were attacked coming here. By someone named Glaan Cabalor."

Cylene senses a movement among the Council members, an uneasiness that settles over them.

"Someone," Parras continues, "didn't want us to come here, didn't want us to try and stop this war. If we find him, we'll have the key to where Valentine's son may be."

Beliathys seems to smile. "That is arranged easily enough. Glaan, step forward."

One of the Metamorphs, one standing near the back, comes close to Beliathys. "Glaan is a revered member of our council. There can be no truth in your accusation."

But Cylene is staring right at him, and all of a sudden everything is clear to her. The glimmering city, the Ghayrogs, a great hall where Glaan Cabalor stands talking, laughing, drinking wine with the Ghayrogs, while before them stands the small fair-haired son of Valentine.

*Turn to section 94.*

# * **84** *

Parras quickly raises his sword. The cook yells over to his two assistants. "Get some guards! Quick!"

They flick their tongues excitedly, even as the cook takes a step back from Valentine.

## THE GHAYROG COOK

*To hit Parras: 11      To be hit: 13      Hit points: 7*
*Damage Done: Knife 1 D6 − 1*

*If Parras hits first, he can remove the knife from the cook and stop his assistants. Turn to section 92.*

*If he is hit by the cook, the fight will go on as the assistants run out. If Parras is still battling the cook after three rounds, turn to section 85. If he should kill the cook before then, turn to section 97.*

*If Parras should die, turn to section 29.*

## * 85 *

The cook proves to be more than adept at handling a knife. Just as Parras is about to force the cook to yield, the kitchen door bursts open and guards enter, surrounding Parras and Cylene.

"Drop your weapon," a Ghayrog commands, and Parras, sensing the futility of it all, lets it slip from his fingers.

"This way," the Ghayrog orders.

"Where are you taking us?"

"To Duke Sarion," the Ghayrog answers laconically.

*Turn to section 98.*

## * 86 *

Their search for Valentine's son, and his captors, could end here if they are arrested, Parras knows.

Perhaps they could run and escape to the jungle.

And perhaps get killed doing so.

## Section 87

Or maybe Cylene could learn something, something that would tell them if any of the Metamorph Council is involved in the foul plot to bring war to Majipoor.

But he must act fast!

*Return to section 90 and have Parras make a different choice.*

## * **87** *

We have a name, Parras thinks. The name of the person who tried to kill us. Could that someone be in the Metamorph camp, and, if so, can Parras expose him before the Council?

But, to do that, Parras would have to trust that the Council itself hadn't kidnapped Brynamir.

*Return to section 90, and make another choice.*

## * **88** *

"The Duke invited us to inspect his storage room, my friend. Of course, if you'd rather discuss the matter with him, I'll be glad to go tell—"

The cook eyes Parras and Cylene carefully, noting their haughty expression. Then, with a snort and a flick of its tongue, it says, "Very well. The room is not prepared for any tours, mind you. But suit yourselves."

Parras smiles warmly.

"Why thank you. We'll be sure to tell the Duke of your help."

*Turn to section 96.*

## * **89** *

*Roll 3 D6 and compare it to either Parras' Intelligence or Wisdom.*

*If Parras should decide to rely on his instinct and the total is the same or less than his value for Wisdom, turn to section 95.*

## Section 90

*If Parras should rely on his intelligence and the total is the same or less than his value for Intelligence, turn to section 86. If the roll is greater, return to section 90 and make another choice.*

* 90 *

*There are a number of things Parras and Cylene could do. Select from the list below. Some choices will allow Parras to return to try other actions. Other choices will be final, sealing Parras and Cylene's fate for the rest of the quest.*

*If Parras and Cylene know the name of whoever sent the assassin to attack them in the caravan, turn to section 87.*

*If Parras decides to tell his mission to Beliathys and the Council, turn to section 93.*

*If Parras wants Cylene to probe the Council members with her psychic power, turn to section 82.*

*If Parras wants to rely on his instinct or Intelligence, turn to section 89.*

*If Parras should decide that they must make a run for it, off the hill and into the nearby jungle, turn to section 81.*

# * **91** *

Parras looks at the Council. "We have none, save our presence here to try to prevent a war. Somewhere, Lord Valentine's son is prisoner, and there is precious little time left for him to be found. Soon, the Coronal will have no choice but to send his troops into the reservation."

Beliathys looks at the other Council members and shakes his head.

"I don't know what you expect us to do, or believe. We must talk about this among ourselves."

*Return to section 90. Decide another action that Parras should take.*

# * **92** *

Parras brings his sword down on the Ghayrog's arm, making him drop his knife. Then he turns and faces his two wide-eyed assistants.

"Hold it right there." They stop, and move

next to the cook, a foul smell filling the room.

"Cylene, see if you can find something to tie them up with."

Cylene looks under the counter in the cabinets until she finds some frayed rope. "It doesn't look very strong," she says, "but it will have to do."

She ties the Ghayrogs to a large black post that stands in the center of the kitchen. Then she runs over to Parras.

"Good," Parras says. "Now, let's get moving. They cost us some precious minutes."

*Turn to section 96.*

* 93 *

"We have to tell them why we're here," Cylene says urgently. "It's the only way."

"Very well," says Parras. "Most esteemed council," Parras says, hoping that he was sounding adequately respectful, "my friend and I are on a mission from the noble Coronal, Lord Valentine."

A few Metamorphs seem to stir, a grumbling coming from them.

Parras pauses for a second and then continues. "Lord Valentine's son has been kidnapped." The Metamorphs gasp in shock. "And the note carried demands supposedly from the Piurivar."

"No," Beliathys shouts. "Lies! There is no truth to this, this *trick*! It will be an excuse for Valentine to wage a final war on the people of Piurivar. We have had enough!"

"No," Cylene pleads, running over to Beliathys, taking his pale hand. "Can you believe that of me? Can you think that the two of us would enter the reservation to merely tell you a lie?"

"Then where is your proof?" Beliathys asks.

*If Cylene and Parras know the name of the person who sent the assassin against them, turn to section 83.*

*If not, turn to section 91.*

## * **94** *

"It's him," Cylene says, extending her arm and pointing at a shapeshifter standing off to the side.

"Glaan Cabalor?" Beliathys says, startled by the sound of her voice. "What are you saying?"

Cylene steps forward, her arm still raised, pointing at the shapeshifter. "He sent an assassin to kill Parras and me. He has been to the crystal city of the Ghayrogs."

## Section 94

"Dulorn?" Beliathys asks quietly.

"To drink and eat with them while sealing the fate of Majipoor. He knows where the Coronal's son is."

"Absurd," the one called Glaan says loudly. "The ravings of a mad Human. Let us lock them up and be done with it."

And Beliathys stands there, indecisive, waiting for the next turn of a card.

Cylene fixes Glaan with her eyes. "Last week, he vanished for two days. And then returned here." She turns to Beliathys. "Is that not right?" Cylene demands.

Beliathys seems to think for a second and then nods. "I believe so, but—"

"And a week before that, and then many, many more times he has disappeared. Is that not true?"

The Council members begin muttering amongst themselves. And then, Parras notices, Glaan seems to take a step backward.

"Yes," Beliathys says. "It is as you say. And where do you say Glaan was all these times?"

"Fools!" Glaan shrieks. "How can you listen to this young woman's babblings?"

But they are listening, Parras notices. And, for the first time, he feels hopeful.

"With the Ghayrogs," Cylene says quietly. "Making plans to sacrifice your people in a war over Majipoor."

The move is slight, almost imperceptible. But

to Parras, who has been in many battles, its intent is clear. Cabalor was going for an energy thrower under his cloak.

"Watch it!" Parras yells, but then the weapon is out, ready to fire.

"Believe an outsider, you will? Listen to her crazy ravings? Well, I'll not stand here like a fool and be abused. I'll settle their fate now."

An icy stillness settles over the depression as everyone watches Cabalor raise his weapon and point it right at Cylene.

Then Beliathys moves, a smooth gesture as he tosses his dirk almost casually but unerringly toward Cabalor. The renegade Metamorph turns, sees the knife flying at him, and realizes it's too late to dodge.

The knife hits Cabalor in the shoulder and he drops his weapon. Some guards from the periphery rush in and grab him.

"You fools," he screams, "it's too late. Within days, the time will have elapsed and the Coronal will send his soldiers to eliminate the reservation."

"Enough," Beliathys says. "Take him to Bilfen. We will question him there."

Beliathys walks over to Parras and Cylene. "You have done us a great service. With your help, war may still be avoided."

"If there's time," Parras says. "If there's time."

\* \* \*

## Section 94

Entering Bilfen is like opening a crumbling, ancient book from Majipoor's past, Parras thinks.

Here Parras could see small houses clustered together, connected by narrow stone paths that wander this way and that. The largest building that he could see was a mere three stories tall, and it was filled with weather-beaten carvings depicting Metamorphs building, farming, and fighting. And all around them, as they moved through the sprawling town, shapeshifters gathered together, to stare at the Council members and then to point at the Humans walking beside them.

Beliathys had said that they would return to Bilfen to eat. But he also hinted that they would be able to learn of the rest of the plot from Cabalor.

"There are ways known to the Piurivar," Beliathys says, "ways of learning the truth."

As they walk the smooth, stone streets, Parras sees Cylene walking beside Beliathys. And he is surprised to feel his jealousy rise, a quick flash of heat that he struggles to douse. Whatever happens, he tells himself, he must remember his purpose here. Everything else is unimportant.

Soon they come to a building slightly larger than the others. Beliathys guides them in and Parras sees that a table has been set with an assortment of fruits, meat and a dark bread.

"I recommend the bread," Beliathys suggests.

"It's made out of the scarlet bulbs of mud lilies, and it has a rich, spicy flavor."

Hungrily, Parras reaches down and picks up a thick slice. "Thank you," he says between chews, "it all looks most appetizing."

"I will be questioning Cabalor and, when I have learned what I need to know, I will return. Until then, rest."

Beliathys leaves, and Parras snatches up great handfuls of the food.

"You must be a bit hungry," Cylene laughs.

"You could say that. And you? Aren't you going to eat some of this wonderful stuff?"

"Yes, later perhaps." And Cylene's face takes on a faraway look that causes Parras to pause in mid-chew.

"Beliathys was your lover?" Parras asks matter-of-factly.

Cylene turns to him. "No . . . I mean, yes, we were lovers. Many years ago. But I couldn't grow to love his Metamorph form. It was too . . . difficult."

"But when he changed—"

"Yes, then I could see him for the strong and good creature that he was. Then I could love him." She walks over to Parras and, when she looks down, he knows that she understands how hard it is for him to hide his jealousy. "But that was a long time ago, Parras. I don't regret it. Just as I don't regret meeting you."

Parras smiles then, extending a forkful of salad to her, a lively mixture of greens native to the area with a creamy herb dressing that has Parras' tastebuds running amuck. "I could retire to a life of ease if I could sell this dressing on the Mount." Cylene takes a bite. "Ummm. Perhaps I *will* fix myself a plate."

They sit together, feasting on the small banquet before them, touching and laughing, renewing unspoken promises.

Later, Beliathys enters quickly, startling them.

"Incredible," he says. "I have just heard the most incredible tale of my life. And though it must be true, I still can't make myself believe it." Then, with a look at Parras and Cylene, "We are in great debt to you, and your brave Coronal."

"What is it you have learned?" Parras asks, wiping his mouth.

Beliathys sits across from them. "Have you ever seen Dulorn?" They both shake their heads. "As a Council member," Beliathys continues, "I have been there a few times. Of course, by simply changing his appearance, a Piurivar could go there any time he wanted. But these times I went as an official representative to discuss trade with the Duke of Dulorn.

"It is, quite simply, a city unlike any on the planet. Its size, of course, is well known, stretching two hundred miles right in the middle of the Dulorn Rift. All the buildings are made out of one approved material, a feather-light calcite

that has allowed architects to let their imagina-
tions roam. And so there are spires and towers
of immense magnitude, reaching almost into
the clouds. And arches that seem to defy gravity,
stretching from one immense structure to another. And, throughout all, the most wondrous
display of decoration, with enormous domes
and balconies of every design.

"Fourteen million inhabitants live in the great
city, most of them Ghayrogs. And the glimmering crystal wonder is ruled over by Duke Sarion."

Parras feels himself growing uneasy as he
recalls his recent dream. The crystal city. The
Ghayrog dressed in a red, red robe.

"It is Sarion who has Brynamir. It is Sarion
who wants war."

Parras' mouth falls open. "But that's crazy.
His army, as large as it is, would be no match for
the forces of the Coronal," Parras says.

"Of course," Beliathys agrees. "If he fought
against the Coronal. But that is not his goal."

"A second Coronal," Cylene says quietly, almost sadly.

Parras turns to her. "A second Coronal? What
do you mean—"

"Listen, Parras," Beliathys interrupts. "There
have been those who claim Majipoor is too
large, too diverse for one ruler. At various times
in our long, troubled history, there have been
those who suggested that the two large conti-

nents should be two separate countries. Zimro-el would become its own world, with its own Coronal."

"What does this have to do with that notion?" Parras asks.

"Duke Sarion wishes to be that ruler."

And here, Parras looks at Beliathys, impressed at whatever method he used to get the information from Cabalor. "His plan could work one or two ways. In the unlikely event that Lord Valentine would willingly withdraw his soldiers from the continent, that would free Sarion to quickly gain control of Zimroel, forging alliances with some races, eliminating others. By the time Castle Mount was ready to return, the new Coronal would be securely in power.

"Or, as is more likely, if Lord Valentine sent massive troops to crush the supposedly rebellious shapeshifters, after the war the troops would linger, to preserve the peace after such a bloody conflict. It would not be difficult for the powerful Duke Sarion to gradually gain control of these troops, in the interest, supposedly, of keeping down rebellion. And then, when he felt his control of troops secure, with their leadership firmly in his grasp, he could have himself declared Coronal of Zimroel."

"But wouldn't Lord Valentine prevent that?" Cylene asks.

"Perhaps. If he wished a bloodbath to rival

what you call the Metamorph Wars. More likely he would decide to let Majipoor be split asunder, since the war would almost be too terrible to contemplate."

Parras interrupts. "I must tell Valentine immediately and he—"

"No, you must not. First, your message might be picked up and that would lead to Brynamir's death. But more importantly, you won't be believed."

"But of course Valentine will—"

"Yes, Valentine will. But his advisors will claim it is merely a shapeshifter trick. Without evidence, they will argue to attack the most likely group, they will argue to attack us."

"Then," Cylene asks, "what can we do?"

"You and Parras," Beliathys says, his eyes almost registering compassion, "must save Brynamir."

"What!" Parras shouts. "How can we save the boy? He could be anywhere in Dulorn, or outside it, for that matter."

"Oh, he's inside it, inside the palace." Beliathys reaches over and fills their wine goblets. "Listen to me, and I will tell you how you will save your beloved Majipoor . . ."

Parras is sitting by himself, watching as the wagon moves out of the reservation.

The most direct route to Dulorn is through the Stiamot Pass, Parras knows, and then to head west toward the Dulorn Rift.

It will be new country for Parras, but he will travel quickly. And, for the entire journey, he will be with Beliathys and these other Metamorphs.

As a plan, Beliathys' idea seems dangerous, perhaps impossible, Parras thinks. But, he realizes, it offers the only hope for saving Brynamir.

He and Cylene will travel with the shapeshifters, into the great city, to be hidden by them in their wagons. The Metamorphs will then schedule an audience with the Duke to discuss certain matters of trade. At that meeting, Parras and Cylene will appear, and Cylene will probe the Duke to discover where Brynamir is hidden, while the Metamorphs hold him prisoner.

Then they will have to move quickly, rescuing the boy and escaping the city. A signal to Valentine should bring enough troops to the city to paralyze any action from Duke Sarion.

If he's left alive, Parras thinks.

So, a plan to be sure. And, perhaps, an impossible one.

Parras tries to not let Cylene's closeness to Beliathys upset him. She sits by him now, as they cut through the dark cliffs of the Longhar Range and move quickly west.

Instead, he busies himself studying the changing terrain, as the low hills change into a dry, desert-like area. Very little rain falls on this side of the range, Parras knows, and it's only when they get closer to the Great Sea that they will again see fertile land.

And all the time, he thinks of the next day, when they will be in Dulorn. You like challenges, he tells himself. Difficult tasks that demand much.

Well, this will quite simply be the challenge of his life.

The Metamorphs stop traveling well before dark, making camp in a methodical way that Parras finds amusing. It's hard to understand such creatures; they always seem to be thinking of something else, something terribly sad.

And later at night, Parras is pleased when Cylene finally comes to him, lying next to him and pulling him tight.

Morning begins too early, and the Metamorphs seem ready to depart before Parras has even had a sip of tea. "Come," Beliathys encourages him. "We must not waste a moment."

So Parras hops on the wagon, his hair pointing in various directions and his cup of hot tea sloshing around, spilling great droplets on the floor of the fast-moving wagon.

By mid-morning, they could see the city. And Parras, despite his familiarity with the wonders of Castle Mount, is impressed.

"Dulorn," Beliathys says.

They approach the immense city from the east, and every point of it seems to catch the light, sending glowing shafts in every direction. But he doesn't get to see the view for long.

## Section 94

"Quickly," Beliathys says. "Get under that tarp and try to remain still."

"Well, that was our view of Dulorn," Parras says, following Cylene. Then they're in the dark, lying still, listening now to the sounds of the shapeshifters as they talk to each other, and the gentle whir of the rotors underneath them.

"Still having fun?" Parras whispers in her ear.

But Cylene's voice sounds hollow when she says, "If you say we are."

They feel the wagon slow, then come to a stop. Then a slightly pungent smell reaches Parras' nostrils. A Ghayrog guard, he suspects, checking on the Metamorphs' reason for entering the city. Dulorn was a restricted area; no Metamorphs allowed unless on official business.

It's hard for Parras to hear what they're saying, and he begins to worry that something has gone wrong.

Come on, he thinks. Move it. Let's get going.

His fingers reach to his side to feel his sword.

He grows more impatient. Something's definitely wrong. Somehow the Ghayrog suspects something. Then, the wagon lurches forward. And Parras knows that they are safely inside the city.

He waits under there with Cylene, breathing the stifling, fetid air. "I can't wait to get out of here," Cylene says.

"Soon," Parras says.

Again, the wagon slows. They hear the sound

of a heavy door moving, then a tremendous banging as it shuts. Beliathys flips over the tarp.

"What was the problem back there?" Parras asks. "Did they suspect something?"

"No. It was the usual friendly welcome for the dangerous Metamorphs," he says sarcastically. "Quickly, out now. We meet with the Duke in under an hour."

"An hour," Cylene gasps. "We'll never do it."

"You will," Beliathys says, "because you'll have to. Come down and I'll show you the map."

Parras looks around as he gets down. They are in a large room, a kind of workshop space really. With an area for the wagon and a series of small rooms to the side.

"Is this where you usually stay on your official visits?"

Beliathys nods. "Yes. They like us together. And, fortunately for us, they like us nearby. This building connects directly to the Duke's palace. Now come take a look at this."

Beliathys spreads a hand-drawn map out on a small table. Parras and Cylene come and stand beside him.

"We will leave through the door to the side, right here. It leads to the main palace entrance hall, which is very well guarded. There is a staircase that goes to the main hall, where Duke Sarion conducts all his official business."

"Where should *we* go?" Parras asks impatiently.

"Right here," Beliathys says, pointing to a spot near the entrance hall, "there's a passageway. It's used by servants and for deliveries. It leads to the kitchen and ends in the storeroom. At the storeroom there's a shaft leading up through the palace. It should be narrow enough for you to climb."

"Any handholds? Ledges, trapdoors . . ."

"I don't know," Beliathys says. "All I know is that it ends in an opening right in the main hall. We will be there to restrain his guards when you enter. The rest will be up to Cylene."

"And what if there's no way up the shaft?" Parras asks.

"Make a way. We will only be able to talk with Sarion for a limited time. After that, our chance will have ended. Of course, if you meet anyone you must silence them. Do not use your energy thrower, Cylene. It will merely call a horde of Ghayrogs on you."

One of the Metamorphs comes over to Beliathys to ask him something, and Parras turns to Cylene. "I'm sorry, Cylene, this may be a bit more difficult than you bargained for."

"Don't worry, Parras. Just get me up that shaft."

They wait, a short time remaining before they are about to start moving, but the time passes slowly, crawling, until everyone is standing around, waiting for Beliathys to say something.

"It's time," he says quietly. "We'll go first,

then you can make your way to the corridor."

Then, the shapeshifter leads his entourage through the door to the passageway and on to the entrance hall.

Parras waits a few moments.

"All set?" he asks. Cylene nods, and then leans forward and kisses him. "For good luck," she says gently.

And they leave the room.

The dark halls lack the glittering light of the buildings above. Here everything has a damp, raw smell to it, made even more pungent by the weird mixture of smells given off by the Ghayrogs.

They come to the door that leads to the kitchen.

"This is it," Parras says. "Try to look as if we know what we're doing."

"And what if we're stopped?"

Parras ignores her question as he leans down and listens at the door. "It's quiet. Let's try it."

He opens the door and they enter another passageway, dimly lit with the faint smell of cooking food. Parras walks ahead purposely, passing closed doors on the left and right.

"The kitchen must be ahead," he says.

"But someone's going to see us," Cylene says.

"Quite likely."

He comes to another door, directly in front of him, and now, leaning down, he can make out the sounds of Ghayrogs on the other side.

## Section 94

"What now?" Cylene asks.

"I'm thinking," Parras says. And he listens, trying to make out how many there are. "Just three of them," Parras says. "Let's get to it."

He opens the door and strides in.

A tall Ghayrog is standing before a massive steaming pot and he turns quickly and shouts at him.

"Hey! Where do you think you're going? This is a private area, not some spot on the palace tour."

"Oh," Parras says, seeing two other Ghayrogs peeling some kind of vegetable off in the corner. "Just moving through, to the storeroom."

The Ghayrog comes over to Parras, stopping to pick up a knife from the counter.

"Stop right there," he says slowly.

*If Parras should decide to take out his sword, turn to section 84.*

*If Parras should decide to talk some more, turn to section 88.*

## * **95** *

Perhaps, Parras wonders, one of the Council members could be part of the splinter group seeking to start another Metamorph war. In that case, it will be necessary to expose him and somehow get the other Metamorphs to help.

"Cylene," Parras says quietly, "see if you can learn anything about the Council members while I try to talk to them."

Cylene nods her head and begins to concentrate.

*Turn to section 82.*

## * **96** *

"Hurry!" Cylene says to Parras. "The storeroom must be this way."

They leave the kitchen and enter a large room with wide shelves reaching to the ceiling. Here are jars and canisters filled with delicacies from every region of Majipoor, and enormous sacks of grain and dried fruit piled on top of each other.

Parras looks around, searching for the shaft.

"Where is it?" Cylene asks.

"I don't know. Unless it's behind a shelf somewhere, hidden by a case of thokka jam."

Then they hear voices, confused and mumbling, coming from the kitchen. "I'm climbing up there," Parras says, pointing to the top shelves. "Somewhere, there's got to be an opening in here."

"Unless," Cylene says, almost inaudibly, "Beliathys was wrong."

"In that case," Parras grunts as he pulls himself up, "we might as well give up now. There's no way we can go through the main entrance. I'm sure that Duke Sarion has given orders to—"

"They're coming this way!" Cylene says, listening at the door.

Just then, Parras reaches the top shelf. "Here it is! It's narrow, but we'll fit. Quickly, climb up here."

And Cylene scrambles to the top, reaching out for Parras' hand, and he gently hoists her up beside him.

The doorknob to the storeroom turns.

"I locked it," Parras says, "but I'm sure it won't hold them for long." A metal grate covers the shaft and Parras begins pulling it, while below him the doorknob turns back and forth even more frantically.

"Do hurry," Cylene says anxiously.

Then the grate pops off, and Parras places it to

the side. "With luck it will take them a while to find where we went. You go first, Cylene."

"Me? I'm not even sure I can—"

"Just crawl in. It runs straight for a bit, and then it goes up. Just use your feet and legs to press your back against the shaft's walls."

"And if I slip?"

"I'll be there. That's why you're going first."

Cylene crawls into the dark hole, tentatively at first, but then she hears a loud banging on the storeroom door, and she hurries in. Parras follows her. There's enough room for him to turn slightly and replace the grate.

"Don't stop now, Cylene. Just keep moving."

"It goes up," she whispers.

"And a good thing it does. Just remember what I said. Use your legs to press your body against the shaft's walls."

And so she climbs, and Parras can hear the squeak of her legs and back as she wedges herself tightly and begins the arduous slide up.

"I can't do it!" Cylene says, groaning.

"Yes you can. Just don't think about it. Just *go up*. Now, move it!"

And then, almost imperceptibly, she starts sliding her body up, inch by inch, slowly moving through the shaft.

Soon, there's room for Parras to enter and begin his climb.

And that's how it all began, Parras thinks. With a climb. A purposeless activity really; just something to awaken his court-dulled senses.

## Section 96

This, yes, this was different. Here the fate of the planet may rest in the next ten minutes, and this climb.

Then Parras hears a loud sound, as the storeroom door smashes open, and he can hear voices talking quickly, wondering where they might be. With luck, Parras hopes, it will take them just enough time to find the shaft.

"I can't do it," Cylene says again. "My legs are starting to ache. I'm not sure my muscles can hold out—"

"They can," Parras tells her, trying to instill belief into her. "But don't stop moving. It's just as tiring waiting there as going up."

And then she starts moving again, and Parras gives a big sigh.

This, he thinks, is not so hard for him. Of course it would be nice to have a couple of lines to pin to the walls of the shaft. But the climb, well, it isn't all that hard. Cylene, though, was suffering. Just as he found it oh-so-difficult to raise the light sails on the *Dark Sea*. So now she is finding this climb so terribly painful. But we're halfway there, Parras thinks. We're going to make it to the top.

"I'm going to slip," Cylene moans. "I can't hold on any longer."

In the murky light Cylene's body is a black shadow, so Parras can't tell if she is indeed in trouble. "No!" he yells, oblivious to their pursuers in the storeroom below. "You—"

But then she falls, right on top of Parras, a

dead weight that knocks the wind out of him
and nearly causes his knees to buckle.

"I've got you," he pants, Cylene resting in his
lap.

"My legs couldn't hold anymore. They just
went wobbly."

"It's okay. It happens to new climbers all the
time. You hold your muscles tight for so long,
and then you just kind of lose control. But I've
got you now. And I'll get us up."

Yes, a small voice suggests to Parras. Now we
have a challenge, don't we? Now every inch is a
torturous, painful experience, while all the
while Cylene's weight seems to grow, trying to
push him down.

He sweats, and every muscle on his face is
pulled tight.

I can do it, he tells himself.

Then, begging . . . please let me do it.

He slides up another inch, and suddenly his
left foot slips. Cylene feels his body give way,
and she clutches him tightly while he struggles
to hold his place and work his foot back into
position.

Below them, they can hear the voices inside
the shaft itself.

"There!" Cylene says. "I see an opening. It
must be the main hall!"

"Best news I heard all day."

"There's a level area. The shaft turns in. Just
get me a bit higher and I can crawl onto it."

Parras moves a bit more and then, blessedly,

# Section 96

Cylene is off him, crawling through the flat part of the shaft.

Then he reaches it, and he thrusts himself through. The ache he feels in his legs now, he knows, is nothing compared to what he'll feel like later.

"Can you see anything?"

"Yes, the Metamorphs are there and a few Ghayrogs. They are holding goblets."

Parras squeezes next to her, and he sees the Metamorphs, with their backs to him, talking to Ghayrogs.

"We've got them outnumbered, at any rate," Parras says.

"I guess this is where we make an entrance?" Cylene asks.

"On 'three.'" Parras grins. And he and Cylene place their feet next to the grate. "One, two, three!"

And they kick the metal plate and crawl out the opening, trying to land lightly on the polished stone floor. "Now, Beliathys!" Parras calls, even as he flies through the air. He lands smoothly next to Cylene, barely seeing the opulent tapestries that fill the enormous walls of the hall. "Now, indeed," a voice says gently. Parras and Cylene stand expecting to see the Metamorphs move quickly to immobilize the guards. But they stand perfectly still.

"What's going on?" Parras says to Cylene.

But Cylene has already looked around the

room, and she stands there, a defeated expression on her face.

"Look," she says, and Parras turns and sees the hall filled with Ghayrogs, their energy throwers armed and pointing at the Metamorphs.

Beliathys turns, and says to Parras, "I'm sorry. He knew. Somehow he knew."

A Ghayrog dressed in a lustrous red robe strides toward Parras, its eyes glowing with enjoyment.

"Not somehow," he says. "We too have been making use of a psychic. Our good friend Delanir here." The Ghayrog gestures to a gray-haired Vroon standing impassively to the side. "But oh, how rude of me. We haven't been introduced. I'm Duke Sarion. Soon to be Coronal of Zimroel."

*Turn to section 102.*

## * **97** *

The cook slashes at Parras, wielding the knife with a terrifying accuracy.

"Watch out!" Cylene calls as the cook jabs at the air, often coming within inches of hitting him.

## Section 98

But then the cook makes a desperate lunge, and Parras brings his sword around, meaning to disarm the Ghayrog. But the cook turns his body suddenly and Parras' sword cuts into him, leaving a lethal wound. The Ghayrog collapses.

Parras stands there, watching him. "I only meant to disarm him," he says quietly. "I didn't—"

"Come, Parras, we must go. There will be guards soon. You did what you had to."

Yes, what I had to, Parras thinks. Killing just happens to be one of those things that I happen to do well. What a wonderful skill to have. How proud I should feel.

"Parras!" Cylene calls. And he snaps out of his maudlin reverie and runs over to her, toward the palace storeroom.

*Turn to section 96.*

## * 98 *

The Ghayrogs roughly push Parras and Cylene out of the kitchen, and once again into the passageway, leading to the main hall of the palace.

As they climb a broad staircase, they are seen by visitors and dignitaries from every part of Majipoor.

The stairs lead to a broad promenade, flanked by a series of rooms used for banquets and meetings. Art of a colorful, abstract nature fills the walls, and smooth, polished sculptures rest on narrow tables beside the palace rooms.

At the end of the hall, Parras can see the huge, gleaming white doors that surely must lead to the main hall of the palace.

Two overdressed Hjorts pull the doors open, and Parras and Cylene are led in.

"Welcome," a Ghayrog dressed in a lustrous red robe calls out. "We have been expecting you."

"Beliathys!" Cylene calls, and Parras turns to see the Metamorph surrounded by Ghayrog guards, their energy throwers pointing directly at them.

"Oh, yes. You see," the Ghayrog says, taking a step toward Parras, "we were not surprised by your little party. I have availed myself of the psychic abilities of my friend Delanir here." The Ghayrog gestures to a gray-haired Vroon standing impassively to the side. "But oh how rude of me. We haven't been introduced. I'm Duke Sarion, soon to be Coronal of Zimroel."

*Turn to section 102.*

* **99** *

Parras and Polol run west, away from the voices, and reach a broad stone staircase leading up. Parras takes the steps two and three at a time.

"Slow down, Parras. I'm not used to moving my body so exuberantly."

But Parras continues to hurry, and reaches the upper corridor. It appears deserted and he calls out,

"Cylene!"

"Here, Parras! I'm here!" Cylene yells to him, and Parras runs to her cell.

"Quick, Polol," he calls out. "Bring the key."

"I'm hurrying as fast as I can."

Polol arrives and fiddles with the lock. Then it clicks open, and Cylene rushes into Parras' arms.

"I thought it was hopeless," she says softly.

"It was," Parras laughs, "until my friend arrived."

Polol performs a slight bow. But then the voices are in the corridor again, coming now from both sides.

"Trouble," Parras says and he sees a pair of guards coming from each end, their swords drawn.

"Well, I knew this wouldn't be that easy,"

Polol says. "I'll take the east end—"

"And I'll take the west," Parras says, grimly moving toward the guards.

GHAYROG GUARDS
*To hit Parras: 13   To be hit: 10   Hit points: 6*
*Damage with sword: 1 D6*

*Parras will fight two of the guards, while Polol fights the other two. Each guard will attack in order.*

*If Parras defeats his two, turn to section 107.*

*If Parras is defeated, turn to section 29.*

## * 100 *

With the shapeshifters effectively posing as Ghayrog guards, Parras, Polol and Cylene are led up through the labyrinthine dungeon to the glittering opulence of the entrance hall. To all appearances, life continues its normal pattern, with well-connected people milling about, discussing business and politics.

Some take notice of the group being led up the great staircase to the private rooms of the palace. But most continue their conversations, oblivious to any disturbance.

"So far, so good," Polol says.

## Section 100

"The real tests are the guards at the top of the staircase. One word of alarm from them and thirty heavily armed soldiers will be on us in a moment," says Beliathys.

Parras glances around and sees the soldiers that Beliathys refers to. They stand very still, on upper balconies and also on the floor, next to massive pillars that support the enormous roof of the entrance hall.

"I see what you mean," Parras says quietly.

All too soon they are standing before the staircase guards.

"Duke Sarion has requested that the Human prisoners be brought to him."

One of the Ghayrogs looks at a sheet of paper on a small table before him.

"I see no such audience on the Duke's schedule. Perhaps I should check if—"

"The Duke called down directly," says Beliathys. "He wishes to see them immediately. I recommend that you do not delay us."

Incredible, thinks Parras. Beliathys radiates such power, completely believable as a Ghayrog, and his voice carries an authority that one would not soon disobey.

The Ghayrog glances at the guards, and then the prisoners. "Very well, but in the future notify us that you will be coming."

"To be sure," says Beliathys sarcastically, and he roughly pushes the three "prisoners" forward, toward the main hall.

"Where are the Duke's chambers?" Beliathys

asks Cylene in a whisper.

She hesitates for a moment, as if confused by something, then her face brightens. "Up there," she says, gesturing to yet another great staircase. "And," she adds with alarm, "there are more guards."

They take the steps quickly, and soon are face to face with two guards, armed to the teeth.

"We bring the Human prisoners. Duke Sarion has requested—"

"No one may proceed past this point unless approved by the Duke in writing," one of the Ghayrogs growls. A foul stench suddenly rises from the two guards to punctuate their comments.

Beliathys looks at the guards and their weapons, and he notices that the one on the left has his foot near a button on the floor. An alarm, Beliathys realizes.

"The Duke will be angry," Beliathys warns.

"The Duke's order will be obeyed," the Ghayrog answers.

*If Parras should decide to make a sudden attack on the guards, turn to section 101.*

*If Parras should rely on his Intelligence, turn to section 108.*

# * **101** *

"Enough!" Parras yells, and he grabs his sword from Beliathys and swings at the guard to his right, the one with his foot poised to press the button.

*Roll 3 D6 and compare it to Parras' Dexterity.*

*If the total is the same or less than Parras' Dexterity, turn to section 103.*

*If the total is greater, turn to section 108.*

# * **102** *

"It will never work," Parras says quickly.

The Ghayrog's tongue pokes out of its mouth as if in response. "Oh, it will work. You and your shapeshifter friends were the only difficulty."

"And the boy?" Cylene asks.

"Quite fine, though he of course misses his daddy. I may even keep Brynamir here, alive, just as an extra bargaining tool. Despite what you think, we are not barbarians." And here the Ghayrog grows angry, as if remembering some past insult. "No, civilized life in this planet does not begin and end on Castle Mount. I will form a new government, drawn from the many races of Zimroel. We *will* be free of Alhanroel's domination."

"With you as Coronal," Parras says dryly.

"Precisely. But this little audience has wasted precious time. Until all these matters are settled, I'll feel better if you're kept locked up."

Sarion raises an arm, and some guards quickly hurry to his side.

"You know," he say to Parras and Cylene, "it's quite amazing that you got this far. Really. But it was impossible for you to go any farther."

Then he turns to the guards, "Take them away."

*Turn to section 105.*

## * **103** *

With a sudden movement, Parras pushes the guards away from the alarm and the Metamorphs quickly grab them.

"Go!" Beliathys says. "Find Brynamir and bring him to safety. We will stay here."

Then Beliathys tosses Parras a coil of heavy rope. "Climb down the back of the palace. We will protect you."

Perhaps, Parras realizes, to perish there.

"Hurry," Cylene says, pulling Parras away. And they move down the hall.

*Turn to section 109.*

## * **104** *

The Ghayrog fights viciously in the crazed, dark corridor, but he's no match for Parras.

Parras is savage, as he smashes left and right, all the time thinking . . .

It will *not* end here.

We will save Valentine's son.

And soon, for Parras, it's over as the Ghayrog collapses under his blows. The shapeshifters are also fighting well, and despite wounds, they too have defeated the guards.

"I haven't had this much fun in a long time," Polol says. And Cylene gives the Skandar a dismayed glance. "I mean," Polol says abashedly, "the skill of it all. Not the actual fighting. It's the art of—"

But Cylene has turned away. "We must hurry. The boy is in a small room next to the Duke's chambers. He's alive but we must hurry."

"Wait," says Beliathys, and he signals to the other shapeshifters. And suddenly the corridors fill with Ghayrogs. "It will be easier for us to make our way up if we pose as guards escorting prisoners."

"Great idea," says Parras.

"And give me your swords," Beliathys says.

"Now wait a minute," Polol starts to say.

"Do it," says Parras. "We can't very well look like prisoners if we're carrying swords."

"Don't worry," Beliathys says with an amused flick of his forked tongue. "You'll soon get them back."

"Hurry!" Cylene orders. "I sense we don't have much time."

And the shapeshifters begin guiding Parras, Polol, and Cylene out of the dungeon, up to the entrance hall, toward the private chambers of Duke Sarion.

*Turn to section 100.*

## * **105** *

Parras looks around the jail cell, and a tremendous sense of failure overwhelms him.

The cell is a cramped, stone cubicle, adorned only with a wood bench for sleeping and a basin for washing. A small hole in the ground, in the left corner, serves as the toilet.

This part of the dungeon, Parras notices, is not exactly overcrowded. A few of the cells are occupied, but most are empty, their barred doors open, awaiting customers.

Depressing, yes, but Parras knows that's not the reason he feels so devastated.

He failed Valentine. To get this close, albeit with some lucky breaks and the help of the shapeshifters, and then to fail! And what failure. Not just a message that would go undelivered, or a life lost. No, this is a failure on a scale undreamed of. Valentine had entrusted the future of Majipoor to me, Parras thinks, and that trust was obviously misplaced.

Outside, Parras can see puffy clouds dotting a clear blue sky over Dulorn. It would look beautiful to the many Ghayrog residents and the horde of visitors who are in the jewel-like city. And no one would know—

No one would know the immense plot being prepared inside the palace of Duke Sarion.

Parras sits morosely on the bench, hoping, praying that somehow he'll wake up to find it all a dream, but the splintery wood is all too reassuring to him that this is all too real.

He hears steps shuffling his way. After a few moments a Liimen appears, dressed in the grayish-green garb of a prison guard. Parras looks up to the oddly shaped face, looking at the three eyes as they blink and observe him.

He certainly doesn't seem used to prisoners of my rank, Parras notes. But if Zimroel gives birth to another Coronal, he soon will.

The Liimen holds a tray of food, some dried

fruit and two slices of a dusky bread. The Liimen says nothing but sets the tray down on the floor and pushes it through a small opening.

"Thank you," Parras says, picking up the tray.

But the Liimen stares for a second, and then hurries away. And Parras begins eating the meager meal.

He bites at the fruit, an incredibly flavorless and chewy substance. Just looking at the slices of bread, Parras can tell they will test the mettle of his teeth.

Then he hears more steps coming toward his cell, and Parras decides that if it's the Liimen he'll give him back the tray. This kind of meal will improve, Parras knows, when his hunger reaches a more advanced stage.

"What's the matter, friend, our food not to your liking?"

Parras looks up, almost not believing his ears. "Polol!"

"I hope you saved a bit for me, Parras. It's been quite a time since my last meal."

"What are you doing here? I thought that you'd—"

"So what do you think? That Lord Valentine would send you off in the wilderness completely unprotected? No, my friend, he knows you all too well. I've been on your trail now since Piliplok."

"But why didn't he tell me?"

"Well, this way, if you were caught, you wouldn't know I was out there somewhere. No matter if they flavored your food with Mindspell, or had a Vroon search your brain, you'd know nothing. Funny thing, though, you almost lost me. I was about to leave Mayrtria when Valentine showed up and stopped me."

Parras looks down the dungeon corridor and whispers to Polol. "Do you have a key? I've got to get out of here."

"Oh, yes," Polol says, digging a heavy ornate key out of his side pocket. "The Liimen guard seemed more than eager to be tied up and thrown in a cell." Polol opens the door and Parras jumps out, giving a great hug to his Skandar friend. Polol gives Parras a sword. "So Valentine followed us to Mayrtria?" Parras asks, strapping the sword on.

"Yes, and he's here now in Zimroel."

"He's here?"

"Yes, with a small army drawn from the regular troops stationed at Falkynkip and Pidruid. He's waiting for us, and then he'll put Duke Sarion out of business."

"He knows about the Duke?"

"As of this morning he does. It's been pretty easy to follow what's been going on, thanks to you. So as soon as we have Brynamir safely out of Dulorn, he'll handle the rest."

They hear voices coming from the eastern end of the corridor, and Parras touches Polol's shoulder. "We've got to move quickly," Parras says. "Cylene can tell us where the boy is being kept. She's being held in a cell one level up."

"Yes," says Polol. "But we could use your new friends, the Metamorphs, to help us. We should free them first. They must be one floor down, in the lower dungeon."

*If Parras should decide to free Cylene first, turn to section 99.*

*If Parras should decide to free Beliathys and the shapeshifters first, turn to section 106.*

## * 106 *

"We'll be in much better shape with the Metamorphs behind us," Parras says to Polol, and he quickly heads west, to the stairs leading down.

A single Liimen is guarding the area, and Parras easily disarms him and places him in a cell.

Beliathys is the first to come out. "I'm impressed," he says. "I thought that this quest was over."

"Thanks to my friend here," Parras says, gesturing at Polol, "we get a second chance."

The Skandar looks away, seemingly uncomfortable in the presence of so many Metamorphs. "Not all of us are over our prejudices," Parras says quietly to Beliathys. "Quickly," Polol says. "We must get to Cylene."

## Section 106

Parras nods, and leads the group to the upper dungeon. And when they reach it Parras calls out,

"Cylene!"

"Here, Parras! I'm here!" And Parras takes the key from Polol and runs to the cell. He opens it and Cylene falls into his arms. "I thought it was over," she says. "How did you—"

"At your service," Polol says with a deep bow. "Now—"

But then there are voices at both ends of the corridor. Four Ghayrog guards appear to the east, and three more to the west. "One for each of us," Polol says. "There are weapons against the wall, over there," he says, pointing to a spot where the cells begin. "I suggest," he says to Beliathys and the shapeshifters, "that you hurry up and arm yourselves."

As the Ghayrog guards advance on them, they raise their swords for battle.

GHAYROG GUARDS
*To hit Parras: 13      To be hit: 10      Hit point: 6
Damage with sword: 1 D6*

*Parras will have to fight one guard.*

*If he defeats the guard, turn to section 104.*

*If he is defeated, turn to section 29.*

# * **107** *

The Ghayrog guards attack with a viciousness that surprises Parras, and he finds himself stepping backward, overpowered by their two swords.

But then he thinks of failure, thinks of how horrible he felt just a few moments before, and he knows that nothing can be allowed to stop him now.

"No!" he yells, slashing left and right, forcing the suddenly stunned guards to hold their ground. And then, again, "No!" And Parras is a man possessed, burning with a single passion. To save Valentine's son.

In moments, it's over, and Polol comes running to him.

"I see you haven't lost your touch."

"Nor you," Parras says.

"Quickly," Cylene calls. "We must free the Metamorphs and then rescue Brynamir."

"You know where he is?" Polol asks.

Cylene nods. "I probed the Duke when we were trapped. The boy is in a room next to Sarion's private chambers."

"That should be easy to get to," Polol says sarcastically.

Parras leads them down, to the lower dungeon. A single guard watches the dank corridor, and they easily disarm him and toss him into a cell. In minutes, the small group of shapeshifters is free.

"I thought it was all over for us," Beliathys says quietly.

Parras notices that Polol seems uneasy around so many shapeshifters.

"Not with my friend here," Parras says, gesturing at Polol. The Skandar turns away. Then Parras says, whispering to Beliathys, "Not all of us are ready to overcome our prejudices."

"No matter," Beliathys says. And then, he signals to the other shapeshifters, and they change. In seconds, Parras is surrounded by Ghayrogs.

"We will escort you to the Duke's quarters as prisoners. If we're lucky, no one will question us."

"Brilliant!" Parras says, and they hand over their weapons.

And the shapeshifters lead Parras, Polol and Cylene up, out of the dungeon, to the upper corridors, leading to the chambers of Duke Sarion.

*Turn to section 100.*

# * **108** *

Parras swings, and hits the guard. But not before the alarm sounds and dozens of soldiers stream up the stairs.

"Any bright ideas?" Polol asks, after restraining the other guard.

"Yes," Beliathys announces somberly. "We will hold the guards for as long as we can. You get to the boy, climb down the side of the palace, and escape."

Parras eyes the hordes of guards streaming up the stairs and he knows Beliathys and the other shapeshifters will be massacred. "Now!" Beliathys orders. And Parras gives the shapeshifter a look of respect. "All of Majipoor will know of this day," Parras says, and then he darts off with Cylene and Polol. "Here," says Cylene excitedly, coming to a heavy door. "The boy is in here!"

*Turn to section 109.*

# * **109** *

"The door is bolted," Parras says, leaning into it.

"That's what you think," Polol says, moving away from it and then running toward it, throwing his entire weight against it.

The door fails to yield, despite the great Skandar's bulk.

"Wait," he says. "One more try!"

And now he runs even faster, literally throwing himself against the door. And it shatters, ripped off its hinges, out of the frame, and Polol tumbles into the room.

And Parras sees Brynamir. A small, blond boy. Fond of kite flying, it was said. A boy who enjoyed exploring the wild places near Castle Mount, the heavy woods free from the Coronal's gardeners' meticulous attention, where mintuns and bilantoons still could be seen darting about.

The boy looks up at Parras, and even as he runs to him he begins to cry.

"Parras!" he says, filling the room with his small, high-pitched voice.

But then Parras sees another figure, tall, imperial, standing off to the side. Duke Sarion.

"It's quite hopeless," the Duke says. "I've already given the alarm and my soldiers will

©1986

arrive in minutes to dispatch all of you, the boy included."

Polol takes a step toward the Duke. "I think," he says grimly, "that we've heard enough out of you." And Parras quickly shields Brynamir's eyes as Polol makes Sarion's robe glisten with an even darker crimson.

"Come," Parras says gently. "We will have to climb down out of the palace. But you like climbing, don't you, Brynamir?"

The boy nods, nibbling his lower lip, struggling to be brave.

"They're coming, we must hurry," Polol yells out.

Parras leads the boy out into the hall, followed by Cylene and Polol. He can hear the sound of tremendous fighting echoing through the hall.

"We've not much time," Polol says.

"I know," Parras answers, and he runs to the back of the palace, to the delicate stained-glass windows that overlook western Zimroel.

Parras takes the coil of rope and ties one end to a nearby pillar, testing it for strength. And then he raises his sword and smashes the window, sending tiny shards flying through the air. Parras then lowers the line.

"Climb on my shoulders," he says to the boy.

Without hesitation, Brynamir climbs on, his small hands nervously digging into Parras' neck.

"Here we go," Parras says, trying to sound buoyant. "Just like that big old vramma tree in the palace garden. Isn't that right?"

Parras' arms strain to ease himself down. Cylene follows, twisting her legs around the rope and sliding down, taking care not to get too close to Parras.

"I'll stay here," Polol calls down. "In case we get some company."

"No," Parras yells. "Come down, Polol."

Dulorn is below them, a dazzling city oblivious to the terror that Parras now feels.

Polol shakes his head.

"It's an order," Parras yells. "I'll have your head back at Castle Mount if you don't come. Besides, who will guide us out of the town?"

Polol seems to think for a moment, and then, "I don't even know if I can move my fat old carcass down. Well, I'll try."

And Polol joins them, and Parras feels that now, maybe, they will be okay.

"I'm scared, Parras," Brynamir says.

"Almost there. Just a little bit more."

Ghayrog guards suddenly appear at the window and stare down at the escaped prisoners. And Parras knows that Beliathys and the shapeshifters are gone.

He reaches the end of the rope, and a short jump away is the pavement.

Parras lets go, and he lands smoothly, barely ruffling the boy's fine hair.

Then Cylene lets go, another good landing, followed by Polol, who plops and rolls like a ball.

"Now what?" Parras asks.

## Section 109

"To our floater," Polol grins. "Just a few blocks ahead."

They run, drawing odd glances from the crowd that fills the streets.

"Just keep moving," Polol yells. "We're almost there."

They turn a corner, and Polol darts into a small shop that sells medicinal herbs and spices. "An old friend," Polol says, pointing at the shopkeeper, and he takes them to a large back room where the floater sits waiting.

Polol hops on and begins to activate the floater, while Parras hoists up Brynamir. Cylene climbs on as Polol says, "Open the doors." Parras swings open the two large doors that lead to the street outside.

"Here we go," Polol calls, and Parras jumps in, beside Cylene, just as Polol guides the floater out.

They sit on a small hill, right on the ground. Dulorn is visible in the distance, as is the small army of the Coronal's troops moving toward it.

For a while, Brynamir didn't stray from Valentine's lap. He just sat there, burying his head against his father's chest while Valentine stroked the boy's head and planted small kisses on his cheek.

But then Brynamir revived, and he left Valentine to explore the small hill, lifting rocks to search for insects, digging around the dirt, and climbing the small trees that dotted the hillside.

Polol, Parras, and Cylene sit around the Coronal, sipping a delicious blue wine and eating a tray of food that, for the first time, made Parras really believe that he'd once again see the Mount.

"I don't know how to thank you," Valentine says, turning to look at each of them.

"It was Polol who saved us," Cylene says quickly.

Polol shakes his head. "Parras and Cylene discovered where your son was, Lord Valentine. All credit goes to—"

But they see Parras shaking his head. "If not for Beliathys, we would never have reached Dulorn. And," Parras says quietly, "we would never have escaped the palace." Parras looks directly at the Coronal. "It was the shapeshifters that saved your son."

Valentine nods. "And maybe more, Parras, maybe more. Who knows what madness might have been let loose had you failed? We owe a tremendous debt to the Metamorphs, one that I will repay. To start with, I will begin by visiting their reservation."

Polol gasps. "A Coronal to enter the Metamorph Reservation?"

"It won't be the first time for me," Valentine smiles. "But that will only be the beginning. Nonetheless, you will always have my endless gratitude as long as I am alive."

"Daddy, Daddy," Brynamir calls from across the hill. "Come look what I found. It's a new bug."

Valentine smiles at the group. "A new bug," he says, standing up. "Well now, that's something I *must* see."

And he walks over to his boy, equal measures of love and pain filling his heart.

Polol glances at the Coronal's army, just now entering Dulorn. "I doubt they'll find much resistance, with the Duke dead and all."

Parras nods. "Most of the city is loyal to the Coronal," Parras says. "It's a revolution that never began."

Cylene leans against Parras, luxuriating in the feel of the soft earth and Parras' shoulder. Polol looks over and then he too stands up.

"I think I'll see if there's any more wine."

And he walks away.

"We've come a long way to get to this quiet hillside," Parras says, looking right at Cylene. "Perhaps we can simply rest and enjoy it for a few minutes more."

Cylene smiles. "My father is waiting for us at Piliplok," she says. "But I'm sure he'll have no trouble entertaining himself for a few more days."

"Nor," says Parras, bending down to gently kiss Cylene, "shall we."

## THE END

©1986

# * **110** *

The following is a list of important locations in the adventure. Only go to a location if you have been to all the previous section numbers.

# A GUIDE TO THE CITIES AND TOWNS OF
## *Revolt on Majipoor*

NOT ALL THE CITIES and towns on the following list can be visited by Parras. While he will be able to enter some in the course of this adventure, others will be places that will play a different role in the course of Parras' quest.

The guide presents the information as known by Parras, which may not be completely untainted by inaccuracies, prejudices, and rumor. Nonetheless, the information contained in these brief descriptions can be most useful in determining Parras' course of action in different situations.

**Bimbak East and West:**
These twin cities, located in western Alhanroel on the lower slopes of Castle Mount, signal the beginning of the farm country of the continent. Due to the many months without rain, the farmers of this region have developed incredible irrigation and water-storage systems that allow year-round farming.

239

**Bylek:**

A small village, nestled in the luxuriant hills below the great Mt. Zygnor on Alhanroel. While its mixed community is fiercely loyal to the Coronal, the villagers are a hearty and independent lot, known for taking the law into their own hands. (Note: not to be confused with the nearby city of Byelk.)

**Alaisor:**

Located on the coast of Alhanroel, Alaisor is the main port leading to the Inner Sea and the continent of Zimroel. It features over a hundred miles of docks, all protected by an artificial harbor.

**Avendroyne:**

The gateway to Ilirivoyne and central Zimroel. It features a magnificent Botanical Garden that weaves its way through the entire city with towering plants brought from all the known worlds. It is the second largest city of the Metamorph Reservation.

**Castle Mount:**

A mountain of cities, home to the Coronal's Castle. The Mount is completely climate controlled, a gentle spring-like weather usually predominating. The actual castle, located at the mountain's peak, rivals many Majipoor cities in size.

**Dulorn:**

A Ghayrog city of incredible beauty. Extending for a hundred miles in all directions, this city's buildings are constructed out of a light, crystalline calcite that has let architects devise the most wondrous towers, spires, and domes. Duke Sorian is justifiably proud of his palace, located in the center of the city.

**Falkynkip:**

One of the trio of cities that dot the western end of Zimroel. Its architecture is rugged and functional, though not without its charm. The human Duke of Falkynkip has historically been an avid supporter of the Coronal.

**Ilirivoyne:**

Located in the middle of the Metamorph Reservation, this is a town composed of wicker shacks that are periodically struck down and moved to a new location.

**Ni-Moya:**

A massive city of over 30 million residents, Ni-Moya is famed for tremendous white towers. Other features include the Gossamer Galleria, a mile-long shopping arcade suspended above the ground by nearly invisible cables, and the Crystal Boulevard. The Park of Fabulous Beasts draws visitors from all over the continent, as does the Museum of Worlds. The Ducal Palace is, at present, not open to visitors.

**Mayrtria:**

The lesser sister to Alaisor, Mayrtria is the somewhat shabby port used by those who cannot afford the more lavish services provided by Alaisor. Despite numerous harbor authorities (most of them Hjorts), the port is known as a gathering place for those involved in illegal activities.

**Pidruid:**

The westernmost city of Zimroel. Pidruid is filled with heavy, lush vines that can be found throughout the city. It is also known, unfortunately, for its roving packs of mangy dogs and prickly-nosed dholes. Common sights in Pidruid include Liimen selling hot sausages on skewers (on nearly every major thoroughfare) and the thousands of tiled-roofed huts, which give off a golden glow in the setting sun.

**Piliplok:**

This city is home to the great dragon ships, the stragely decorated vessels that hunt the sea-dragons. There has been some concern expressed over the fact that some hunters have been slaughtering young dragons, illegally, to cater to a demand among rich patrons. The city itself is organized like a wheel, with its streets the spokes radiating outward.

**Velalisier:**
 The fabulous and mysterious city of the Metamorphs, destroyed at the end of the Metamorph
Wars. It is now a ruins, and is said by some to be
haunted.

# ABOUT THE AUTHOR

Matthew J. Costello is Features Editor at *Isaac Asimov's* and *Analog SF* magazines. He is also a Contributing Editor at *Games* magazine, where he reviews new releases.

Prior to writing *Revolt on Majipoor*, Matt wrote four solitaire role-playing adventures, including a DC Heroes Batman module, *Wheel of Destruction*, and a Role-Aids module for Advanced Dungeons and Dragons™, *Final Challenge*.

His first novel, *The Horror*, will be published by Zebra Books in early 1987.

# CROSSROADS™ ADVENTURES

## THE BEST IN FANTASY

☐ 54973-2　FORSAKE THE SKY by Tim Powers $2.95
　　54974-0　　　　　　　　　　　　　Canada $3.50

☐ 53392-5　THE INITIATE by Louise Cooper　$2.95

☐ 55484-1　WINGS OF FLAME　　　　　　　$2.95
　　55485-X　by Nancy Springer　　　　Canada $3.50

☐ 53671-1　THE DOOR INTO FIRE　　　　　$2.95
　　53672-X　by Diane Duane　　　　　Canada $3.50

☐ 53673-8　THE DOOR INTO SHADOW　　　$2.95
　　53674-6　by Diane Duane　　　　　Canada $3.50

☐ 54900-7　DARKANGEL　　　　　　　　　$2.95
　　54901-5　by Meredith Ann Pierce　Canada $3.50

☐ 54902-3　A GATHERING OF GARGOYLES　$2.95
　　54903-1　by Meredith Ann Pierce　Canada $3.50

☐ 55610-0　JINIAN FOOTSEER　　　　　　$2.95
　　55611-9　by Sheri S. Tepper　　　Canada $3.50

☐ 55612-7　DERVISH DAUGHTER　　　　　$2.95
　　55613-5　by Sheri S. Tepper　　　Canada $3.50

☐ 55614-3　JINIAN STAR-EYE　　　　　　$2.95
　　55615-1　by Sheri S. Tepper　　　Canada $3.75

☐ 54800-0　THE WORLD IN AMBER by A. Orr $2.95
　　54801-9　　　　　　　　　　　　　Canada $3.75

☐ 55600-3　THE ISLE OF GLASS by Judith Tarr $2.95
　　55601-1　　　　　　　　　　　　　Canada $3.75

Buy them at your local bookstore or use this handy coupon:
Clip and mail this page with your order

**TOR BOOKS—Reader Service Dept.**
**49 W. 24 Street, 9th Floor, New York, NY 10010**

Please send me the book(s) I have checked above. I am
enclosing $_____ (please add $1.00 to cover postage
and handling). Send check or money order only—no
cash or C.O.D.'s.

Mr./Mrs./Miss _____

Address _____

City _____ State/Zip _____

Please allow six weeks for delivery. Prices subject to
change without notice.